"Where's your sense of adventure?"
Travis asked, as his mouth returned to
Josie's for another heart-stopping kiss.

She didn't want to think beyond how wonderful he made her feel. But common sense won out, and she called a halt to the craziness. "Whoa, cowboy, I think things are getting out of hand."

Travis smiled. "And this is a

"Yes. We've both ips."

"So, what's w

She gave him a

"Don't you see, ued, "you and I have no secrets."

Josie tried not to look guilty, knowing Travis had a knack for reading her. How would he react if he discovered her secret? She didn't want to know. She wasn't foolish enough to think anything serious could happen between them. A few laughs and some kisses shared with a good-looking man. As long as she remembered that, one day…soon, she would have to pack up and walk away.

Problem was, could she handle that?

Dear Reader,

I hope the long hot summer puts you in the mood for romance—
Silhouette Romance, that is! Because we've got a month chock-
full of exciting stories. And be sure to check out just how
Silhouette can make you a star!

Elizabeth Harbison returns with her CINDERELLA BRIDES
miniseries. In *His Secret Heir,* an English earl discovers the
American student he'd once known had left with more than
his heart…. And Teresa Southwick's *Crazy for Lovin' You*
begins a new series set in DESTINY, TEXAS. Filled with
emotion, romance and a touch of intrigue, these stories are
sure to captivate you!

Cara Colter's THE WEDDING LEGACY begins with
Husband by Inheritance. An heiress gains a new home—
complete with the perfect husband. Only, he doesn't know it
yet! And Patricia Thayer's THE TEXAS BROTHERHOOD
comes to a triumphant conclusion when *Travis Comes Home.*

Lively, high-spirited Julianna Morris shows a woman's
determination to become a mother with *Tick Tock Goes the Baby
Clock* and Roxann Delaney gives us *A Saddle Made for Two.*

We've also got a special treat in store for you! Next month,
look for Marie Ferrarella's *The Inheritance,* a spin-off from
the MAITLAND MATERNITY series. This title is specially
packaged with the introduction to the new Harlequin continuity
series, TRUEBLOOD, TEXAS. But *The Inheritance* then leads
back into Silhouette Romance, so be sure to catch the opening
act.

Happy Reading!

Mary-Theresa Hussey

Mary-Theresa Hussey
Senior Editor

Please address questions and book requests to:
Silhouette Reader Service
U.S.: 3010 Walden Ave., P.O. Box 1325, Buffalo, NY 14269
Canadian: P.O. Box 609, Fort Erie, Ont. L2A 5X3

Travis Comes Home

PATRICIA THAYER

SILHOUETTE *Romance*

Published by Silhouette Books

America's Publisher of Contemporary Romance

If you purchased this book without a cover you should be aware that this book is stolen property. It was reported as "unsold and destroyed" to the publisher, and neither the author nor the publisher has received any payment for this "stripped book."

To Hence Barrow,

A special man who taught a California girl about ranching
and the love of Texas. I'll always treasure our visits,
the great stories, but mostly your friendship.
You were my inspiration for this series. Can't wait
for your 100th birthday party. Save me a dance. Love, Pat

 SILHOUETTE BOOKS

ISBN 0-373-19530-3

TRAVIS COMES HOME

Copyright © 2001 by Patricia Wright

All rights reserved. Except for use in any review, the reproduction or utilization of this work in whole or in part in any form by any electronic, mechanical or other means, now known or hereafter invented, including xerography, photocopying and recording, or in any information storage or retrieval system, is forbidden without the written permission of the editorial office, Silhouette Books, 300 East 42nd Street, New York, NY 10017 U.S.A.

All characters in this book have no existence outside the imagination of the author and have no relation whatsoever to anyone bearing the same name or names. They are not even distantly inspired by any individual known or unknown to the author, and all incidents are pure invention.

This edition published by arrangement with Harlequin Books S.A.

® and TM are trademarks of Harlequin Books S.A., used under license. Trademarks indicated with ® are registered in the United States Patent and Trademark Office, the Canadian Trade Marks Office and in other countries.

Visit Silhouette at www.eHarlequin.com

Printed in U.S.A.

PATRICIA THAYER

has been writing for the past sixteen years and has published fifteen books with Silhouette. Her books have been nominated for the National Readers' Choice Award, Virginia Romance Writers of America's Holt Medallion and a prestigious RITA Award. In 1997, *Nothing Short of a Miracle* won the *Romantic Times Magazine* Reviewers' Choice Award for Best Special Edition.

Thanks to the understanding men in her life—her husband of thirty years, Steve, and her three sons (along with her new daughter-in-law)—Pat has been able to fulfill her dream of writing romance. Another dream is to own a cabin in Colorado, where she can spend her days writing and her evenings with her favorite hero, Steve. She loves to hear from readers. You can write to her at P.O. Box 6251, Anaheim, CA 92816-0251.

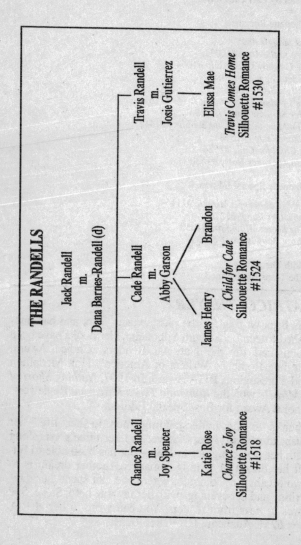

THE RANDELLS

Jack Randell
m.
Dana Barnes-Randell (d)

Chance Randell
m.
Joy Spencer

Katie Rose

Chance's Joy
Silhouette Romance
#1518

Cade Randell
m.
Abby Garson

James Henry   Brandon

A Child for Cade
Silhouette Romance
#1524

Travis Randell
m.
Josie Gutierrez

Elissa Mae

Travis Comes Home
Silhouette Romance
#1530

Chapter One

Travis Randell reined in his horse as they approached the rise. He drew a long breath to help slow his breathing from the hard ride and looked out at the incredible lush green view of Mustang Valley.

A rich blue sky topped the line of long grass waving in the warm breeze. Shrubs and huge oak trees dotted the landscape like soldiers protecting their land. They also sheltered the small herd of mustangs the valley had been named for, and twenty years ago, the three misfit Randell boys who had come to live on the Circle B.

Removing his hat, Travis used his shirtsleeve to wipe the sweat from his forehead. Texas in October. The early morning heat was surprisingly intense, and he'd ridden his mount pretty hard. Not a good idea, but Rocky was just as eager as he was for the race. As a kid, Travis could outride both his older brothers. Chance and Cade had thought he was just plain crazy.

Maybe he was. Maybe that was how he lost everything, or maybe it was because he'd let himself trust. Not an easy trait for a Randell. But he had, and paid the price. All his dreams had gone up in smoke.

Hell, he was going to make his first million before thirty. He'd succeeded all right, but lost it even faster. And no matter how far or how fast he'd ridden, he couldn't outrun the pain and shame that plagued him. Once again the family name had been tarnished, and he'd caused it.

Travis climbed off his horse, and taking the reins, led the roan gelding toward the creek. He crouched down, scooped some water in his cupped hands and drank thirstily. After having his fill, he stood, leaving Rocky at the stream and went to sit under a tree.

Travis had been back at the Circle B for two weeks, and if it hadn't been for Ella, he'd still be hiding out in his old bedroom. He smiled. Even when he'd been a kid, the Circle B housekeeper would never let him brood. She said it was a waste of time. Early this morning, she'd pushed him out of the house and told him she didn't want to see him back until dinner.

Sadness coursed through him as he thought about the past month. How had his life fallen apart? All the years of school, work, the planning and sacrifices he'd given up to start his computer security business, Private Access. It was history now. It was gone. All because he'd trusted a woman.

Damn! How could he let himself be taken in? He thought he was too smart. Hell, maybe he would have seen it coming if he'd been thinking with his brain and not his... He shook away the thought of Lisa's expert seduction. Next time he'd be ready.

God help the woman who tries it again.

The sound of a voice interrupted his thoughts.

Travis cocked his head and listened. Someone was singing. A soft, husky woman's voice floated through the air. He stood. There wasn't supposed to be anyone around. Certainly not on Circle B land.

Angered by the invasion, he followed the sound toward a group of shrubs about a hundred yards up the creek and stopped suddenly when his gaze locked on the grove of trees. There was a clearing and a campsite under them, a sleeping bag, and a backpack. And the trespasser.

A woman sat on a large rock beside the creek, her back to him as she leisurely brushed her hair. Something stopped him from calling out to her. Instead, he watched the rhythmic actions of the brush running through the long silken strands as the filtered sunlight danced on her beautiful raven hues.

Then Rocky's whinny broke the spell, and Travis glanced back to see that the horse had followed him. The sound also caught the intruder's attention. She swung around and stood.

"Who's there?" she called out.

The woman was tiny. She couldn't be any more than five-two or three and probably not a hundred pounds. Her green-hazel eyes were large and haunting as she stared back at him in challenge. Her obvious Spanish heritage was only enhanced by the coal-black hair that flowed halfway down her back. Dressed in faded jeans and scuffed boots, she looked like she belonged on a ranch. But not this ranch. He tensed as he glanced down at her sleeping bag and spotted the camera.

Dammit. They'd found him.

Travis stepped out into the clearing. "I think you

already know who I am. Now, you've got one minute
to get the hell off Barrett land.''

Josie Gutierrez opened her mouth to speak, but at
the mention of the Barrett name, she suddenly lost
her voice. This cowboy with the brooding dark eyes
wasn't about to let her explain. His cowboy hat was
cocked back, revealing light-brown hair that fell
across his forehead. He was tall with wide shoulders.
His large hands were fisted on narrow hips.

Josie knew she'd better do something fast because
he wasn't going to give her much time to explain.
And she hadn't had time to think up a story. Seeing
this cowboy's seething look, she knew no matter what
she told him, he wasn't going to believe her.

"Barrett land?" she said.

"Don't play innocent with me. You know damn
well where you are."

"I just came here to take some pictures of the valley."

"You're lying," he accused, then walked to her
camera, but before he could reach it, Josie grabbed it
away, holding it protectively. She'd worked too many
fourteen-hour shifts to pay for her camera. No one
was going take her prize possession.

"No really, I'm just interested in the scenery and
the mustangs. Is there a law against that?" she asked,
trying not to back away from him. Don't show fear,
she told herself.

"There's a law against trespassing."

"I didn't think anyone would mind. I was just
camping for the night. And I was going to clean up
my mess. Sorry if I intruded on your privacy. I'll
leave now."

He stepped in front of her. "Not until you give me the film in your camera."

"What?" The man was crazy. "I told you I took pictures of the landscape and the mustangs."

"Cut the bull, Ms.... Do you have a name?"

"Josie Gutierrez."

"Ms. Gutierrez. I'm not buying it." He held out his hand. "I want the film."

"And I'm not giving it to you. I'm a photographer. I sell my pictures."

"And you trespassed on private property to get those pictures."

"Is this your land?" she asked, knowing from her limited research that Hank Barrett owned the Circle B.

"I don't see that it's any business of yours."

She straightened to her full, five-foot-three height. "Well, is it? You could be trespassing, too. How do I know that you aren't a cattle rustler?"

The man's jaw tensed. His eyes flared with anger, then turned hard. "Who the hell sent you? What newspaper do I contact when I have you tossed in jail?"

Before Josie could deny anything else two men on horseback came over the rise. One man was about thirty, but her breath caught when she saw the other was in his sixties. Could he be...?

They rode down to the trees. The older man spoke. "Travis, what's going on?"

Travis faced the rider. "Not sure, Hank. I found her camped here. I was just getting rid of her."

Josie's heart began beating wildly. He was Hank Barrett. She couldn't take her eyes off him as he climbed off his horse. He was tall, with straight broad shoulders. His face was weathered from age and the sun, but it was his eyes that made her stomach tighten. Hank Barrett had hazel eyes...like hers.

He walked toward her and smiled. "Hello, Miss, I'm Hank Barrett." He tipped his hat. "And this is Travis Randell, and this is his brother, Chance." Hank removed his gloves and held out his hand.

She gave the three of them a tense smile. "I'm Josie Gutierrez." She took his hand.

"Sorry Travis hasn't been very neighborly. I know there are several campgrounds in the area. Is there any particular reason you decided to camp here?"

Travis threw up his arms. "Isn't it obvious? She's here to get a picture of me."

Josie had had enough of the man. "Get over yourself, Mr. Randell, I don't even know you." She looked back to see a broad grin on Hank's face. "I just take pictures of wildlife and scenery, Mr. Barrett."

"Please, call me Hank."

Her heart tripped again. "Hank...I heard about Mustang Valley and thought I could get some good shots. I'm trying to make a living as a photographer."

Chance Randell climbed down from his horse and joined them. "Are you here to work on the guest ranch brochure?"

Josie swallowed and mentally asked for forgiveness for her next lie. "Yes, I want to work on the brochure," she replied. "I haven't made a name for myself as a photographer, yet. I mean, I haven't published anything that you would know about. So I thought that if I took some pictures of the valley you might like my work."

"It's a lie, Hank," Travis insisted. "She's more than likely from a Houston newspaper."

"I've never been to Houston in my life." That was the truth.

Hank held up his hands. "Why don't we go back to the ranch and sort this out over breakfast?"

"She's just trying to con you, Hank," Travis said.

Hank looked at Josie. "Josie, would you please come back to the Circle B so we can talk this out?"

There was no turning back now. Josie turned away from Travis's furious glare. "I'd like that, Hank."

"Good. Now how did you get down here?"

"I hiked," she said. "My car is up by the road."

"You hiked down here?"

She nodded.

He smiled and shook his head. "Travis, you stay and help Josie pack up and see that she gets back to her car, and then to the ranch."

"But, Hank…"

The older man's gaze locked with Travis's. The look they exchanged was brief, but it told a lot about the respect and love that Travis had for Hank—and that the feelings were returned. Josie felt a twinge of envy. Then Hank turned to her and smiled. "I look forward to our breakfast together, Josie."

Josie nodded and watched as the rancher climbed back on his horse and rode off with Chance. She felt her eyes mist. He was not what she'd expected. But how would she have known what he'd be like?

She'd never met her father before.

Travis was still fuming when he arrived back at the ranch with Josie Gutierrez following behind him in her beat-up red Volkswagen. No matter what, he still didn't believe her story. Her pretty hazel eyes might have fooled Hank, but not him. She wasn't even a good liar, and he knew women who were experts. He'd bet his share of the ranch Ms. Gutierrez had a secret agenda. And he was going to find out what it was.

He directed her to park by the back door while he rode Rocky to the corral, then asked one of the hands to take care of the horse. He headed toward the house where Ms. Gutierrez waited on the small back porch. Hank came out just before Travis hit the step and escorted her inside.

Travis walked through the door to the mudroom, then into the kitchen just as Hank was introducing Josie to Ella. The Circle B's housekeeper had a big grin on her face. Travis didn't like it.

"Well, well, it sure is nice to meet you Josie. And welcome to the Circle B. I hope you're going to be staying around awhile."

Travis took his place at the table. "After the pictures are developed I doubt she'll be here very long," he announced.

Hank ignored him and offered their guest a seat next to him. "Our breakfasts here are pretty basic, Josie. I hope you like bacon and eggs."

"That will be fine. You're very kind to invite me," she said.

"Just being neighborly," he said. "What do you do when you aren't taking pictures?"

"My mom and I used to run a small diner. I've done everything from waitressing to filling in as a short-order cook."

Hank's eyes lit up. "Is that so? Do you have any specialties?"

"Well, let's see." She looked thoughtful. "Our corned beef hash and biscuits and gravy were pretty popular with the regulars."

Hearing Hank's envious groan, Travis had to bite back a grin. For more than twenty years, the Circle B men had been subject to Ella's limited cooking skills. Instead Ella had perfected her ability at being the best substitute mom for three teenage boys.

They all loved the no-nonsense woman in jeans and a plaid shirt. She wore her gray-streaked hair short, and her kind eyes glowed with love. It didn't matter if she could cook or not.

The food was set on the table. "Thanks, Ella," Travis said.

"Thank you," she answered with a smile. "I guess I should have thrown you out sooner. You always did bring back the most interesting things."

Before Travis could explain, the housekeeper moved on.

Hank started the conversation. "Josie, where you from?"

"El Paso."

Hank nodded, then got a faraway look. "I used to travel there years ago…cattle business. So you came to San Angelo to look for a job?"

Josie had trouble swallowing her food past the lump in her throat. "I don't think I'll be going back," she said. "My mother passed away recently, and she was my only family there."

"I'm sorry," Hank said. He set his fork down and reached for her hand; immediately she felt the warmth in his touch. "That's rough. You have any other family?"

"Not that I'm that close to," she said, catching his

curious look. "I was thinking about starting over somewhere else. I want see if I can make a go of it as a photographer."

Travis knew he didn't want Josie hanging around the ranch. Since the news of his business's crumbling became public, the media had been having a field day over his misery. He'd already been humiliated enough when the police had questioned him over the security leak traced to Private Access. He also recalled how the Houston papers had used him as their whipping boy. So he wouldn't put it past them to have sent someone here to the ranch. Hadn't he been humiliated enough? Did they have to continue to hound him, too?

No, he didn't trust anyone with a camera. And definitely not a woman. He knew firsthand how devious women could be. They worked their way into your confidence, only to use you to get what they wanted.

He looked across the table at the beautiful Ms. Gutierrez. Something told him she was harboring her own secrets. And he was going to make sure he found out what they were before anyone got hurt.

Two hours later, Josie knew she should leave, but Ella seemed eager to get her corned beef hash recipe. She also knew that the housekeeper was playing matchmaker. Travis's name had been mentioned more times than she could keep count. Somehow the woman missed seeing that Travis had loathed Josie on the spot.

Seated at the kitchen table, Josie looked up when another man came through the back door. He had to be a Randell. He looked a lot like both Travis and Chance, but his hair was darker, and he was a little taller than his brothers. He smiled at her as he removed his hat.

"Hi, I'm Cade Randell," he said.

"I'm Josie Gutierrez."

"I hear my little brother tried to evict you today."

She blushed. "I shouldn't have been in the valley. It's just that I wanted to see it, and I thought it wouldn't hurt to stay the night. I'm sorry."

"I'm sure whatever Trav put you through was enough punishment."

"He was just being protective."

"He's being ornery, but that's another story," Cade said with a wave. "I hear you want a chance to take the pictures for the guest ranch brochure."

"Yes, but I haven't had a lot of experience."

"My wife, Abby, and I aren't hung up on experience. We want to catch what Mustang Valley is really about. Do you have any samples of your work?"

Her heart raced with excitement. "I have a few photographs in my car. I'll go and get them." She stood and hurried outside. Maybe this could be the break she needed. If not, she definitely had to find a job. She had less than three hundred dollars, her mother's small insurance check to her name, and in her condition, she would need more than that. She had to find work, fast.

She lifted a small album off the seat and was closing the car door when she came face-to-face with Travis.

"Oh, sorry," she apologized. "I didn't see you."

He glared at her, as if trying to intimidate her. "Just so you know, I'll be watching you. So you'd better be careful. You could take potshots at me all you wanted in Houston, but I'm not going to let you hurt my family. Do you understand?''

Josie caught the flicker of pain in his dark eyes. She recognized the look. Someone had hurt Travis Randell and hurt him badly.

"I don't know what you're talking about," she said. "I'm not here to hurt anyone, Mr. Randell. I swear.'' Just herself, if Hank found out her real reason for being here.

"Make sure you keep that promise, or you'll answer to me.''

He stepped out of her way and allowed her to pass. Josie drew a long breath as she increased her pace, but suddenly felt light-headed. She grabbed hold of the porch railing, and waited for the queasiness to pass. She swayed and closed her eyes as her legs weakened. Suddenly she felt hands against her back, Travis's. Then he gripped her by the arm and guided her to a chair on the porch.

"Put your head down," he ordered. With a gentle nudge, he pushed her head down between her knees.

"Give it a minute and you should be feeling better.'' His voice was gentle, soothing.

Josie felt scared. This had never happened to her before. After a few minutes, she raised her head slowly. "I'm okay.''

"Well, at least, your color is back.'' His dark gaze locked with hers. "You shouldn't be running around in this heat, especially if you're not used to it.''

She was used to the heat. What she hadn't expected was this man's kindness. She studied his face and saw his honest concern for a stranger, a side of Travis Randell that surprised her.

But she couldn't depend on it. If he discovered her

real reason for being here, there's no telling what he'd do. "I'm much better, thank you." She stood and once again his expression turned hard. Turning away, she walked inside the house.

The cool air hit her as she entered the kitchen where Cade was waiting for her. She handed him the book, then sat down while he went through each page. She found she was nervous at his scrutiny. She didn't want to get her hopes up about this job. Getting it would mean she'd be able to spend more time here and could see Hank Barrett again. Her stomach fluttered. Was that too much to hope for?

"Josie, these pictures are wonderful." Cade looked up and smiled. "I'd like to show them to Abby if that's all right with you? She'll be coming by soon."

"Of course," Josie said, then drew a needed breath. "If you like I could develop the pictures I took in the valley this morning and get back to you."

Just then Hank walked into the room with a tall woman with auburn hair. Smiling, she leaned down and kissed Cade. "Did I hear my name mentioned?" she said.

"Abby." Cade stood and drew her into an embrace. "I want you to meet Josie Gutierrez. She's a photographer who wants to apply for the job of creating our brochures."

Abby smiled and extended her hand. "Nice to meet you, Josie."

Josie shook it. "Nice to meet you, too."

"I hear your peaceful morning was interrupted by my brother-in-law," Abby said.

Josie felt her cheeks redden. Had the whole area heard about the confrontation between her and

Travis? "I'm guilty. Sorry, I should have asked permission first."

Hank stepped forward. "And I probably would have given it to you, especially if you turned that pretty smile of yours on me."

They all laughed. Josie couldn't believe how nice they were being to her. Well, not exactly everyone. "Let me drive into town and have the film I took this morning developed. I can bring the pictures back this afternoon."

"Sounds like a plan," Cade said. "We'll be here all day."

Just then Ella came in. "Then plan on stayin' for supper, Josie. I always have plenty."

"Only if you let me help prepare it," Josie countered.

"You got yourself a deal," Hank said with an eager smile.

Josie said her goodbyes and left. She was heading for her car when she heard Travis's voice.

"Leaving so soon, Ms. Gutierrez?"

She stopped but told herself she wasn't going to let him goad her. "Yes, I'm driving into town."

"Do you need any directions? Wouldn't want you to get lost again and end up on private property. A person could get shot."

Josie had had enough. Travis Randell didn't trust her. She had a feeling it wasn't just her, but her entire gender. And if he found out the real reason she was here, he'd get rid of her for sure.

"I'm never going to convince you that I mean you no harm. But I need this job." She saw the stony gaze on his face and knew she wasn't getting anywhere. "So, expect me back."

Before she could climb in the car, he grabbed her arm. "Don't threaten me, lady. I'm about at the end of my rope with your kind. You see, I know firsthand what an aggressive woman can do when she wants something. I lost nearly everything I've worked for because I trusted one. It won't happen again. The only thing I have left is my family, and by God, you better not hurt them. Do you understand?"

"Yes," she said and jerked away. Trembling, she managed to put on her seat belt, and start the car. After shifting into first gear, she started down the road to the highway. Tears welled in her eyes, but she refused to let them fall. Not over a guy like Travis Randell. He wasn't worth it. But darn it, he had everything she had always wanted. A family.

Josie shifted into second gear, picking up speed as she glanced in her rearview mirror. He was still watching her. Why wouldn't the man just go away? She looked back at the road but not in time to find a cow blocking her way. She hit the brakes but knew it was futile. She couldn't stop in time. When she jerked the wheel to avoid the collision, her car veered off the road onto the dry grass. A scream escaped her as the car bumped over the rough terrain toward the huge tree. Oh, God, she was going to crash. All her thoughts turned to her baby as the impact threw her forward into the windshield and pain coursed through her body. Then everything went black.

Travis raced for the truck the second he saw Josie's car heading for the Hereford. His heart was pounding wildly as he hurled down the road praying he could help her, but he'd seen her car go into the tree and knew she couldn't walk away. At the scene, he jumped out of the truck and raced to the wrecked car and yanked open the door. His pulse went into overdrive when he saw Josie's limp body against the steering wheel.

He gently nudged her. "Josie. Josie, come on, darlin' wake up."

He got a moan for his efforts.

Carefully he pulled her back against the seat. He brushed wayward strands of hair from her pale face. "Come on, Josie, wake up." He stroked her soft cheek. She moaned again, then finally her eyelids fluttered as she clutched her stomach. "My baby. Please, don't let anything happen to my baby."

Chapter Two

Josie's head hurt but not as badly as her ankle. She opened her eyes. The sudden light caused her to blink, but she ignored the brightness and glanced around the stark-white room. Where was she? she wondered.

Oh, God, what happened? Her thoughts flashed back to Travis's soothing words promising her that she was going to be okay as he had lifted her out of the car. Then in the truck, the sound of his voice drifting in and out as he drove down the road.

Josie tried to sit up, but the pain in her head intensified and she groaned.

Suddenly Travis Randell appeared beside her. "Take it easy there," he said as he helped her lie back down.

"Where am I?"

"A small hospital just outside San Angelo."

A hospital. She didn't have any money for a hospital. "I can't stay here."

He leaned over the bed, so close she could see the

golden flecks in his eyes. "You haven't any choice, Josie. You could be seriously injured."

Panic raced through her as her hand moved to her flat stomach. "Oh, no."

His gaze was understanding, but he said nothing. Did he know? "Is there anyone you want me to call?"

"No, there isn't." Sadness filled her. Since her mother's death all her family was gone, except for Hank...and the baby.

"What about your baby's father?"

Heat flooded her face as she glanced away. "What are you talking about?"

"The baby you're carrying," he said. "It was your only concern when I reached you after the accident. How far along are you?"

"What are you, a doctor?"

Once again Travis found himself frustrated by the woman. Her stubbornness would drive anyone crazy. But he couldn't help but wonder what kind of man she loved. What kind of man would let her run off with his child? "I should let the father know where you are."

"No!"

Travis felt his frustration build. "He has a right, Josie."

"No, he doesn't. He gave up any rights when he told me to get rid of it and then left me."

Before Travis could say anything, the doctor walked into the room. "So our patient finally decided to wake up. How are you feeling, Ms. Gutierrez?"

"I hurt," she said. "My head and leg."

"Well, it seems you have a slight concussion, and your ankle took the brunt of the accident. You have some deep lacerations, but the X rays showed it's just a bad sprain. Overall you're a lucky lady."

"X rays!" Alarm race through her. "But I'm pregnant."

He smiled. "The baby is fine. We took all the precautions to protect the fetus."

Josie relaxed against the pillow as the doctor continued to write on her chart. "But Ms. Gutierrez your blood tests show that you are slightly anemic. Prenatal vitamins and proper diet should handle that."

"Then I can leave?" she asked hopefully.

"Well, we'd like to keep you overnight for observation."

"But I can't stay," she said anxiously. "I don't have the money to pay for all this."

"Don't worry about that," Travis stated. "The ranch insurance will handle the cost. Besides, it was our fault that the gate was open and the cow got out"

"But I don't want to stay in the hospital," she insisted.

The doctor frowned. "Is there someone who'll take care of you?"

Before she could say anything, Travis spoke up. "She'll be staying at the Circle B. There are three of us who can make sure she and the baby are cared for."

Travis could see by the look on Josie's face that she wanted to turn down his offer, but she wouldn't for the baby's sake. For once, he had the upper hand with this woman, but he knew that wouldn't last long.

Three hours later, Josie was settled in the big bed in the ivory-colored guest room. She felt strange about staying at the Circle B. The last thing she

wanted to do was intrude in Hank Barrett's life. She'd
only planned to come and see the man that her mother
had loved all these years. Josie's father.

But her mother, Elissa Romero, had never told
Hank about the child she carried twenty-five years
ago. Instead, she had married Raul Gutierrez to give
her daughter a father. It hadn't been a happy union.
Although when Raul had wanted to marry the pregnant Elissa, and promised that his love would carry
over to her baby, it hadn't. He couldn't handle a child
of mixed blood with hazel eyes. A constant reminder
that his wife had loved someone else. Raul had never
been physically abusive, but his cutting words had
hurt Josie and her mother.

Maybe that was the reason Elissa Gutierrez had
given up so easily when she had been diagnosed with
cancer. Even all Josie's prayers had failed to instill in
Elissa the will to live. She was too weak to fight the
fatal disease, and Josie lost her. But there had been
one thing she had given her daughter before her death.
She had revealed the name of her father.

The soft-spoken, widowed rancher from San Angelo, Hank Barrett.

Tears formed in Josie's eyes. She had wanted to
hate her mother for so much, for keeping her father
from her...and for dying. All her life, people had
abandoned her. First her father and now even her
baby's father.

Frank Hobbs had worked on a ranch outside El
Paso. He'd come into the diner one night. Josie had
been working double shifts during her mother's ill-
ness. It wasn't long before his good looks and charm
worked on Josie, and they began to date. But Josie's
first concern was her mother and a career in photog-

raphy. Frank only wanted her in his bed. The night of her mother's death, Josie had turned to Frank, and they ended up making love. And making a baby.

"I'm just like my mother," she breathed as she wiped the tears off her face. "No, I'm worse." She hadn't even loved the man she had given herself to so easily. And Frank was grateful that she didn't want to marry him. There was one thing Josie was sure of, she wanted this baby. She already loved her or him. The baby had been the reason she'd come to San Angelo. She needed to see her biological father, to form some connection between him and the child. But by the looks of things, with Chance, Cade and Travis, Hank Barrett had all the family he needed.

A knock sounded on the door, and Travis walked into the room, carrying a tray. "Hi," he said.

"Hi," she answered. A warmth traveled through her body as she watched the good-looking man come toward her. He had showered and changed into a pair of new jeans and a starched blue shirt. His sandy-brown hair was damp, falling over his forehead, making his espresso eyes stand out.

"I hope you're hungry," he said. "Joy, Chance's wife, along with Abby and Ella are downstairs cooking up a storm. That's a good thing because it isn't safe to leave Ella alone in the kitchen."

"But isn't she the cook and housekeeper here at the ranch?"

He actually smiled at her. "It's a long story. I'll tell you when you're feeling better."

She was having trouble with his sudden kindness. "I will be gone by then."

Travis set the tray down on the bed and drew a calming breath. Why did this woman have to be so argumentative? He glanced at her wrapped ankle and the bag of ice resting on top of it. She wasn't going anywhere—not anytime soon. Besides, she didn't have a drivable car.

His gaze returned to her face. Although still a little pale, Josie Gutierrez was strikingly beautiful. Her long dark hair was braided and hung down her back, while strands of curls had sprung free and circled a heart-shaped face. Large green-gray eyes revealed a lot, sadness and fatigue. As much as he wanted to deny it, he couldn't help but feel a kinship with her. She looked as lonely as he felt. And although it would be wiser to send her away, he couldn't.

Not when he'd been responsible for her accident.

"Let's wait a few days and see how you feel," he suggested. "Now, eat. That's orders from the kitchen."

She stared at the big bowl of stew, green salad and homemade biscuits. "I can't possibly eat all this."

"Just give it a try," he suggested. "I can guarantee it's good. Besides, I can't face the ladies downstairs unless you've made a dent in some of that food."

This woman didn't give in easily. He watched her finally pick up the spoon and dig into the stew. He held his breath until two large bites disappeared. "Oh, don't forget your vitamins," he said as he reached for the bottle on the bedside table. He handed her a pill, then held out a glass of milk.

She took a long drink, then made a face. "I hate milk."

"Well, you're going to have to change that, because the baby needs it."

Josie's spoon played in the stew. "Does everyone know about the baby?"

He shrugged. "Ella saw the vitamins. If you think they're going to judge you…"

Her hazel eyes locked with his in a fiery stare. "I've been judged all my life," she said. "I was just concerned about my chances for the brochure job."

Travis hated to admit he'd been wrong about Josie. She hadn't been a photographer from a Houston paper. While he'd been waiting at the hospital, he'd looked at her driver's license, telling himself that he might need to contact family. Josie Gutierrez's home address was in El Paso.

His mistake made him feel like a heel. He grimaced, remembering the cruel things he'd accused her of. He'd tried to chase her off the ranch out of vengeance. He was damn lucky that she hadn't been seriously hurt.

"Look, we've all been judged at one time or the other." Hell, he didn't want to think about how his situation was affecting the family. "If your pictures are good, then Abby and Cade will hire you."

"If I don't get that job, I'll need to find something. What about my car?" she asked.

"Your car is fine," he lied. "I'll handle it myself."

"I have insurance, but the deductible…"

He raised a hand. "I said, I'd handle it." He headed for the door, then paused. "Now finish that dinner and get some sleep. If you need anything just holler. My room is right next door." Before she could protest, he walked out. But he knew he hadn't heard the last from Josie Gutierrez. To his surprise, he was looking forward to the next time.

After dinner, Travis went out to the backyard patio. The evening was still warm as he took a seat at the table to enjoy some peace and quiet—something that had escaped him since he'd been home. But maybe Ms. Gutierrez's crashing into their lives would draw attention away from him. Ella sure was crazy about having another person to care for. But how long was their house guest going to be around? The doctor wanted to recheck her ankle in five days. She couldn't leave before then. Not without her car. He'd had it towed to a body shop, praying that the battered vehicle wasn't going to be totaled. He knew that Josie was traveling with limited funds. She'd hadn't minced words when she told him she needed a job.

Earlier, he realized that Josie wasn't as tough as she tried to make people think. He could see the fear in her eyes. She was pregnant. And alone. He shook his head. How could a man not want his own child?

Travis tensed. He knew firsthand not all people were cut out to be parents. His mother, Dana Barnes-Randell, was great, as much as he could remember of her. But not his daddy, that was for sure. Hell, Jack Randell couldn't stay out of trouble long enough to take care of his boys. The man hadn't thought twice about what was going to happen to three sons when he got sent to prison. Chance, Cade and Travis had been lucky, though. Hank Barrett had come along and taken them in. For twenty years the widowed rancher had been the only father that they'd known, or claimed.

Travis leaned forward in the chair and rubbed his hand over his face. He hated like hell that his trouble had brought scandal to the Randell name once again. Over the years, he and his brothers had worked hard to erase the stigma attached to it. His father had brought shame to the Randell name and now so had Travis.

Chance had become one of the top quarter horse breeders and trainers in Texas. Cade had gone to Chicago and made his name in the financial world, before coming home to marry his college sweetheart and to claim his son.

And the youngest brother of the family, Travis had gone to college and worked in the computer field. Then a few years ago he'd started his own business. Last year Private Access was on its way to being one of the premiere computer companies in the country. Once Travis had his software patented, there wasn't going to be any stopping him. He was going to the top. He had even found the woman of his dreams and planned to be married.

Life couldn't have been any sweeter, until one day a month ago when it all came crashing down. It had been bad enough that his fiancée, Lisa Kyles, had been carrying on with his partner, Byron Neeley. But more was going on. Suddenly his clients were beginning to complain about security leaks. It had taken Travis a few weeks of searching, but he'd finally found the problem. For a price, Byron had allowed a competitor access to highly confidential files. It had to be his partner, because he was the only other person with the ability to break into the system.

By then Travis had to involve the police, and his files were confiscated. Even worse and more humiliating, the press got ahold of the story. Travis had been hounded for weeks. He was ruined, and Byron and Lisa were nowhere to be found. Knowing he couldn't handle things on his own, he'd turned to his family.

But was it such a good idea to drag his problems home?

Hearing voices, Travis looked up to find Hank and his brothers coming to join him.

"That was a great dinner Joy cooked," Hank stated.

"Beef stew is one of my favorites," Chance agreed and rubbed his flat stomach. "I think I've put on weight since we've been married."

"I wasn't going to mention it...." Cade teased and Chance playfully punched him in the arm. "Hey, I'm only telling the truth."

"Like you aren't as happy as a dog with a bone."

The two brothers shared a smile.

"Well, as far as I'm concerned," Hank began, "I'm grateful to Joy and Abby for sweetening your dispositions. You weren't fit to live with before."

"Well, the right woman will do that," Cade said.

Travis glanced away. Both his brothers had gotten married this past summer. Although he was happy that Chance found Joy and Cade found Abby, it was difficult to be around all their wedded bliss.

"You didn't eat much, Trav," Chance observed.

"I guess I just wasn't hungry. But tell Joy I liked her stew."

Chance smiled. "I'll be sure to do that. What's on your mind, bro? Anything we can help with?"

He released a sigh. "Yeah, turn my life back about six months. And make me a whole lot smarter about choosing a business partner...and a woman."

Cade pulled his chair closer. "I would if I could, but we can't, Trav. But maybe we can help fix it."

Travis raised an eyebrow. "How?"

"I know a private investigator who might be able to dig up some answers," Cade continued.

Travis shook his head. "No, the two people with the answers are long gone. Byron and Lisa are probably out of the country by now, along with a lot of money."

"Doesn't hurt to try," Chance said. "Not if you want to clear your name. Not to mention fight those lawsuits."

Travis shot out of the chair. This was a nightmare. Private Access had been his life. It had taken off. With his know-how, and Byron's marketing skills, they were going to take the computer world by storm. Now everything was gone. He could never recover that momentum.

"I have nothing left, Cade," Travis said. "They took all the assets, ruined my credibility. You can't run a security business without people's trust."

"But it wasn't you that sold out," Hank said. "It was Neeley, and he has to be held responsible. Go after him, son. This guy Cade knows is the best. If anyone can find them, Alex Rucker can. He specializes in computer technology fraud."

Travis hated not being in control. It was just like when he was a kid, and his older brother got him out of messes. Well, he wasn't a kid anymore. And he did still have a little pride left.

"Look, I appreciate y'all wanting to help. But if it's all the same to you, I'd like to do it myself."

Both his brothers nodded as if they understood. "You think I could have this Rucker's number?"

Chance pulled out his card from his pocket and gave it to Travis. "Had a feeling you'd want to handle it yourself." He got a smile. "Don't worry about the cost, this guy works for a percentage of the recovery.''

Travis studied the card. That gave him some encouragement. But he had little hope of getting back what he really wanted, his reputation. ''Thanks, I'll let you know what happens.''

Hank spoke up. ''We're here for you, Travis. Just don't lose the sense of who you are and what you've worked to become. Your name is important. All you boys struggled hard to overcome what your daddy did. I know you don't take this lightly, Travis, and we're just glad you've come home to let your family help you out. We will stand by you no matter what.''

Travis swallowed the lump in his throat as he looked around the table to see his brothers nod in agreement. God, he'd missed this. ''Thank you.''

''You're doing the right thing, Trav,'' Cade said.

He nodded. ''Yeah, I know. It's just that I feel lost. I've worked twelve-hour days for so long…and now nothing. I feel so useless.''

''Oh, are you going to be sorry you said that,'' Chance said. ''We've been letting you take it easy these past weeks. We have plenty to keep you busy, especially since we're trying to open Mustang Valley Guest Ranch by spring.''

''Hey, I'm not a rancher.''

''You used to be,'' Cade said. ''And believe me, it will all come back to you when you're in the saddle for a few hours.'' When Travis tried to speak, Cade raised his hand. ''I think I remember a kid brother who could ride us both into the ground. So don't give us any sob stories.'' Cade grew serious. ''Really Trav, we need you. And the Circle B is one-third yours now, and not just the ranching part. If we're going to be ready for the retreat opening by April, we need someone to computerize the entire operation and design a Web page to help promote business.''

Travis felt his mood lifting. Maybe this could be a new beginning. At least it was a start. His thoughts went to the woman asleep upstairs in the guest room. Someone else needed a start, too. What was Josie going to do if she didn't get this job? How was she going to take care of her child?

"Before I build a Web page, I'll need some pictures of the valley. Have you had any other offers to do the brochure?"

By the half-hidden smiles on his brothers' faces, he knew they weren't buying his innocent question. Cade spoke up. "Abby likes Josie's photos. But I was hoping to get a look at the pictures she took of the valley."

"Why don't I take the roll in tomorrow and have it developed, then you can decide?"

"Sure. We're going to have to move quickly on this. Abby wants to send the brochures out to some travel agents."

"I'll talk to Josie."

"How is she feeling?" Hank asked, unable to hide his concern.

"Her ankle hurts, but she's too stubborn to admit it. She doesn't like having to stay here."

Hank frowned. "Are you giving her the impression that we don't want her to stay?"

Travis shook his head. "No. I know now I was wrong to treat her like I did."

"It takes a big man to admit his mistakes."

"And to see that the woman is a real looker," Chance added.

Travis felt the heat rise to his face. "I bet Joy would love to hear how you feel."

Chance scooted his large frame lower in the chair. "My wife doesn't have to worry, she knows exactly how I feel. But a man can't help but admire beauty."

"Is that so, Mr. Randell?" Joy asked as she came through the door, carrying her sleeping six-month-old daughter.

"I'm in big trouble," Chance joked as he stood and went to his wife. He kissed her, then took the baby.

His wife smiled up at him. "You can be saved if you take me home and convince me I'm the only woman in the world for you."

"My pleasure," he said.

Everyone wandered into the house, and saying their goodbyes, Cade gathered Abby, and their seven-year-old son, Brandon, and they all walked to the trucks. Hank, Ella and Travis waved them all off and returned to the house. Ella retired to her living quarters next to the kitchen while Hank and Travis headed for the stairs.

"I'm glad you changed your attitude about Josie," Hank said. "She seems nice. And with a baby on the way, she's going to need friends."

Travis agreed, but just her presence here was going to be distracting for him. "She was worried what we'd think about her being pregnant."

Hank shook his head. "Assure her that she's welcome to stay here as long as she needs to recover. After all, she was hurt on the property."

Travis nodded but didn't know if it was a good idea that Josie stay here. Not when even he felt obligated to help her. He knew all too well about women in need. That had been how he'd met Lisa. She'd come to Private Access to answer an ad for a secretarial job about a year ago, and although she wasn't qualified, he'd hired the pretty blonde. Now, looking back, he wondered if she'd planned to use him from the beginning. Travis had learned the hard way not to trust so easily...again.

He stopped at Josie's room and listened, then opened the door and stepped into darkness. With only the moonlight to light his way, he walked to the bed, telling himself he was there to check on her condition.

He studied the pretty woman asleep on the pillow. She looked so peaceful he hated to wake her, but he leaned over and touched her shoulder. "Josie..." he whispered.

She made a moaning sound, then opened her eyes and gasped. "Travis?"

Her husky voice sent warm shivers through him. "I need to check your eyes."

"I'm fine."

He sat down on the edge of the bed. "Do you have to argue about everything?"

"No," she said as she sat up, then grimaced.

"Your ankle still hurt?"

"A little."

"Do you need something for the pain?"

She shook her head. "No, I don't want to take anything because of the baby."

"Of course," he said and glanced down at her flat stomach. She didn't look pregnant. Of course, she was only a few months along, but he couldn't help but wonder how long before she started showing. What would she look like with a rounded belly?

He quickly shook away the thought and picked up

the penlight on the bedside table, leaned forward, and shone it in her eyes, and caught a whiff of her. A fragrance he couldn't describe other than it was Josie. Somehow he managed to check to see if her pupils were dilated—they weren't.

"You're fine. Do you need anything?" he asked.

"I'm okay. Really," she said as she rotated her neck.

"Your neck sore?"

"A little," she admitted.

Without thinking about the consequences, he placed his hands on her neck. A warmth shot through him as he silently worked the tight muscles in her neck. He didn't want to think about the silky texture of her skin, or how close he was to her. But when she released a quiet whimper, he couldn't take any more.

"That should help," he said and stood. "I'm close by if you need me, and I'll be back in a few hours to check your eyes again."

She opened her mouth to argue, but this time he placed a finger over her lips. Another mistake. They were so soft, so warm. "I can be more stubborn than you, Josie. So accept the fact that we're here to help you."

She sighed in resignation.

He started to turn away. "I forgot. I was wondering if I could take your film in to be developed. Abby would like to see the pictures you took of the valley."

"Sure," she said, and pointed to the dresser. "My camera is over there."

Travis retrieved the top-of-the-line 35mm camera and handed it to her. Josie hit the rewind button, then popped open the case, pulled out the roll of film and gave it to him.

"I'll take good care of it for you," he promised.

"Thank you."

"As Hank would say, 'just being neighborly.'" He walked out of the room, his pulse still racing like a sprinter. Damn. He refused to let another woman get under his skin.

part of it was the crowd packed on the side of that one platform that...

...if Renee Cook came off the porch, he grabbed... "Thank you."

As Hank would say, "Just doing my duty." He walked out of the room and out and taken the a porch. Cade... He turned to ten another woman and...

Chapter Three

A large yellow glow brightened the blue sky as the sun started to peek over the distant hills. Hank leaned against the porch railing, enjoying the incredible view. This had always been his favorite part of the day. Dawn.

He took a hearty sip of Ella's coffee. The woman couldn't cook to save herself, but she did make the best brew around. He smiled, knowing that she was the happiest he'd seen her in years.

That was because all the boys were home.

Hank wasn't feeling too bad about it, either. Although Chance, Cade and Travis weren't really his, he always thought of them that way. Since the day he'd taken them in and given them a home, they'd been like his own boys. Although Cade and Travis had been gone for years, they were home now.

And two of those supposedly wild Randell boys were settled now. Chance had a wife and a baby daughter. At first Hank thought the boy was just plain crazy agreeing to marry a woman he'd only known less than a week just so he could get ahold of some land. But it hadn't taken long for Chance to fall in love with Joy and little Katie Rose.

Then a short time later, Cade had returned from Chicago. At a party he'd run into Abby Garson, the girl he'd loved since he was sixteen. He started acting as angry as a wounded bear. Then after Cade discovered they had a seven-year-old son together, he'd done everything to get into Abby's life except admit that he still loved her. It had been their son, Brandon, who finally brought them together. Now they're a real family.

And a few weeks ago, the youngest, Travis, had showed up. After a rough time in Houston, Hank was glad that the boy felt he could return home and let them help him.

Oh, yeah, there was nothing like family, Hank thought as he looked around the ranch. He'd spent most of his life building the Circle B. Forty-three years ago, when he'd brought his new bride to San Angelo, he had planned to fill the large ranch house with children. Since he'd been orphaned, Hank didn't have any family, and he and Mae both wanted a large brood. But years passed, and the babies never came. Although Mae had never said anything, he knew how much it bothered her that she couldn't give him a child. He told her many times that it didn't matter, but she was never convinced. When he'd lost his bride at forty-five, his life seemed to fall apart, until Chance, Cade and Travis came to live with him. Too bad Mae had never gotten to know them; she would have loved the boys as much as he did. They didn't need to be blood for him to call them his sons.

And now they were all home again...and then some.

Hank grinned when he thought about the Circle B's newest resident, Josie Gutierrez. The dark-haired beauty reminded him of someone, but he couldn't quite figure out who.

He liked her. What he liked best was how she could rile Travis. That boy sure was in a snit about her being around. Hank shook his head. Good. It was time he thought about something besides computers. He needed a woman who got his blood stirred up. Hank would bet his prize bull that Josie might just have enough spunk to handle a Randell.

"What you all grinning about?"

Hank didn't turn when he heard Ella's voice. "Just thinkin' how lucky I am."

"So what's put that dreamy look in your eyes?"

He sighed. "I was thinking about all the years I've been standing on this porch, looking out at this land." He gave her a sideways glance. "And the boys."

"That should keep you smiling awhile—having them home."

"It does."

She sobered. "Are you worried about what's happening with the ranch? With Mustang Valley?"

"Naw, Chance and Cade are doing the right thing. With cattle prices up and down, we need some security. Not for me, but for them and for the grandkids." He smiled. "Can't say I'm unhappy that they're all so close to home."

Ella crossed her arms. "I guess I'm feeling the same. But what about Travis? I'm thinking he's going to be heading back to Houston when this mess is cleared up."

"I'm not so sure," Hank said. "I don't think he knows either. Maybe our Ms. Gutierrez will hold his interest long enough so he won't want to go back."

The housekeeper smiled. "Why you old codger, are you trying to matchmake?"

"Like you haven't thought about it?" he accused playfully. "Besides, she seems like a nice young woman who's had some bad breaks."

Ella nodded. "Alone and with a baby on the way. That poor dear... I just hope she's good with a camera."

"Something tells me she'll do just fine." After seeing the loneliness in Josie's eyes, Hank knew he couldn't let her leave. She needed a dose of family.

Hank turned to Ella. "Besides, it's fun to watch her rile Travis."

About eleven o'clock the next morning, Travis yawned as he drove the truck back toward the ranch. He'd gotten up twice during the night to check on Josie. Waking the sexy green-eyed woman put ideas in his head that had nothing whatsoever to do with anything medical.

Travis groaned, remembering the soft purring sounds she'd made when he nudged her awake. It had taken all his willpower to do his job and then leave. Travis wasn't a saint but he'd never taken advantage of women.

"They just take advantage of me," he said sarcastically. He turned off the highway and rode under the Circle B archway. No, he wasn't going to waste time thinking about Lisa. She was Byron's problem now. He had moved on. Not an easy thing to do when his life was in limbo.

Travis already knew he'd have to start over, from scratch. But first he had to get out of the mess he was in now. Hopefully, Cade was taking care of that. One thing for sure, he needed his family. He kept remembering what Hank had told him once. He couldn't do anything about how another person acted. It was only his actions that mattered. Although the family hadn't blamed him, Travis had blamed himself. And one way or the other he was determined to clear the Randell name.

He pulled the truck beside the barn and parked in the usual spot. Seeing Hank with one of the hands, Travis grabbed a sack off the seat and went to talk with him.

"You're up early this morning," Hank said.

"I had some errands." He held up the sack. "Josie's photos."

"Are they any good?"

"I don't know," he admitted. "I thought she should be the first one to see them."

"Then let's go find her." Hank walked toward the house with Travis beside him.

In the kitchen, Travis was surprised to see Josie seated at the table, Ella braiding her hair.

"Travis, you made it back," the housekeeper said. "You were gone so long, I thought you were headed back to Houston."

"Not hardly, I just needed to get something taken care of this morning." He turned to Josie. She was dressed in a white blouse and a pair of faded jeans. Her feet were bare, except for her bandaged ankle. His attention returned to her face, and he caught her challenging look. "What are you doing out of bed?"

She shrugged. "I got bored."

"And how did you get down here?"

Her pretty green eyes darted away. "I managed with Ella's help and some crutches."

"I didn't exactly encourage her," Ella said.

Travis figured as much. He glared at Josie. "Don't you realize that you could have fallen? And in your condition…"

Her chin came up. "I can take care of myself, and my condition is not your concern."

"The hel—heck it isn't," he said perhaps a little too strongly.

"No, it's not. I've managed for years," she insisted.

She had to be the most obstinate woman he'd ever met. And by the look in her eyes, he wasn't going to get anywhere. "Fine. Then I've got things to do." He handed her the sack, then walked out.

Josie felt the heat rise to her face. Why did that man have to be so bossy? She glanced at Hank and Ella. "I'm sorry for that. It's not that I don't appreciate everyone's help, but I'm used to doing things for myself."

Hank sat down next to her. "And I raised those boys to be helpful, to treat women with courtesy and respect." He raised a hand. "I don't doubt that you can handle things, Josie, but I do believe Travis feels responsible for your accident."

"He's not," she gasped. "I'm the one who was driving."

"And it was a Circle B ranch hand who left the gate open."

"But I don't blame you or anyone."

Hank smiled at her. "I'm glad to hear that, but humor us males. We just want to take care of you

until you're healed. Now tell me, do you have anywhere else to go?''

Josie shook her head, feeling her tears threaten.
"No…"

His hand covered hers. "Then let us help you."

It was so hard for her to depend on anyone. Now
with her mother gone, there was only herself…and
the baby. "I'll try."

"Good. Now, let's have a look at those pictures."

Josie opened the sack and drew out the stack of
glossy prints, surprised to find that Travis had gotten
her two sets. Touched by his thoughtfulness, she went
through them, examining each photo closely. Some
hadn't turned out as she'd hoped, others showed her
lack of experience, but there were six pictures she
thought captured the early morning beauty of the valley. She only hoped Cade and Abby felt the same.

"How did they come out?" Hank asked.

Josie forced a smile. "Pretty good. I wish I had
taken more than just the one roll." She had planned
to take additional shots before Travis had interrupted
her. At the time she hadn't any idea that her photos
would be the link to her father's life.

She handed the stack of photos to Hank. "I hope
these will be enough to give Abby and Cade an idea
of what I have in mind for the brochure."

It seemed like a tremendous amount of time passed
as Hank scanned the pictures. She found herself anxiously waiting for his approval of her work. After a
few minutes he smiled, causing the lines around his
eyes to deepen. "These are really good. You sure
caught the sunrise. No place is prettier than that valley
at dawn. Oh, Lord, Mae and I used to ride out there
many a morning…" He stopped, his kind eyes took

on a faraway look and Josie knew he was remembering a happy time.

"Was Mae your wife?" she asked timidly.

Hank nodded. "Yes." He sighed. "Lord, she's been gone more than twenty-five years. Must be these pictures that reminded me of her."

"I hope my pictures brought you good memories." Josie stole a glance at the silent Ella, who was looking over Hank's shoulder at the photos.

There were so many questions Josie wanted to ask this man, her father. Did he ever care about her mother? Were those trips to El Paso—to Elissa Romero's bed—just to help him get through the loneliness? Did he know how much her mother had loved him? Would he have wanted his child if he'd known that he left his lover pregnant?

Josie doubted she'd ever get a chance to ask those questions. Travis would make sure she didn't hang around too long. She had a feeling that he would personally escort her to the gate when it came time for her to leave. A sadness swept over her. She had never belonged anywhere. Not in her stepfather's house, and not here.

Travis wanted to kick something, mainly his own backside. He'd acted like a jerk. Why had he let Josie get to him? He already knew she wasn't a reporter digging up dirt. Why couldn't he just leave her alone? Why did he feel threatened by her? Hell, if he knew.

One thing was for sure, she would be staying around awhile. Hank wasn't about to toss the woman out. Not a woman expecting a child. Hank wouldn't do that and neither would he. Still, Travis didn't completely buy the idea that she was here for the brochure job. Had she been just camping and taking pictures of the scenery? Why else would she come to the Circle B? Maybe she was a spy working for another guest ranch. Damn, if he wasn't getting paranoid.

Travis knew one thing, even if he didn't want Josie around, he had to curb his anger. It was one of the bad traits he'd inherited from his father, and he wasn't proud of it. Being that he'd been away from his brothers for years, it had been a while since anyone had agitated him as much as Josie had.

Even Byron and Lisa hadn't caused him the turmoil that Josie had in the last twenty-four hours. And he didn't need it. Not by a long shot.

Best thing to do was keep his distance. Easier said than done, he thought as he headed toward the house. It was too hot to go for a ride. He glanced toward the sky, wishing the rain that had been threatening all morning would come. They needed a good gully washer to cool things off.

He walked into the kitchen to find Josie trying to stand up.

He rushed to her side. "What are you doing now?"

"I thought I'd go back upstairs and rest."

His eyes met hers. "Well, you're not going to walk. Even with a crutch."

"I made it down here just fine. I can hold on to the furniture and railing."

Ignoring her stubbornness, he bent down and swung her up into his arms. "How about I just carry you?"

She gasped. "No, I don't need you to. I can make it fine on my own."

"Ms. Gutierrez, will you stop arguing for a minute," he pleaded. "I'm going to carry you, one way or the other. So shut up and enjoy it."

That was her problem, Josie thought. She did enjoy it. Too much. With a silent surrender, her arms went around Travis's broad shoulders as he walked out of the kitchen. He easily carried her through the dining room, then into the huge living room done in neutral tones where a camel-colored leather sofa and over-stuffed chairs faced a large television. The stone fire-place covered a big part of the wall and was adorned by a carved oak mantel holding a row of pictures of the boys in different stages of growth. Hank's family. If things had been different she might have been in-cluded, too.

Travis carried her halfway up the stairs, then stopped. "Maybe you want to stay down here awhile longer?"

Josie shook her head. She had intruded enough on everyone's life. Doubts about her coming caused her stomach to clench, and her breakfast was threatening to come back up.

"Please, I need a...bathroom," she asked, praying she wouldn't embarrass herself.

"Lord, woman, you're turning green," Travis said as he took the steps two at a time, then stormed through the bathroom door. He set her down. "If you need me—"

"Get out," she cried and pushed at him. He backed out and shut the door just as Josie made it to the commode and got sick.

After the retching stopped, she had just enough strength to rinse out her mouth. Then she sat down on the closed toilet lid. She touched her tender stom-ach. "Well, little one, I guess you mean business."

This had been her first bout with morning sickness, and it wasn't even morning.

There was a soft knock on the door, and then Travis called her name. Josie groaned. Couldn't the man leave her in peace?

The door creaked open and Travis peered in. "You okay?"

"Oh, yeah, just hunky-dory."

Travis came in and picked her up in his arms. Josie didn't have the strength to fight him. In fact, she welcomed his strength, his ability to take charge. Just for a little while she wanted to lean on someone else. Just once she wanted someone to take care of her.

He murmured soothing words as he carried her into her room and placed her on the bed. Leaning over her, he pulled a cotton throw up around her shoulders. "You rest awhile," he said.

"Just for a minute," Josie said, feeling like she'd been drugged. Her eyelids drooped. The last thing she saw was the crooked smile on Travis Randell's face. It was beautiful.

Later that day, Travis sat in the kitchen with Cade and Abby looking over Josie's pictures.

"These are really good," Abby said. "She captured the valley at the perfect time. In the morning with the dew on the grass. It's beautiful. What do you think, Cade?"

"I agree, honey. I also like your idea. Breakfast in the valley. Who wouldn't want to wake up to this on vacation? I'd like waking up to this."

Abby gave him a pouty look. "Hey, I thought it was me you liked waking up with."

"It is, sweetheart, but wouldn't the valley make a great honeymoon retreat?"

She gasped. "I could work up a honeymoon package, and I bet Joy could figure out some menus for the newlyweds. Like a champagne-and-omelet breakfast and sunset suppers. Oh, it's a great idea." She kissed her husband.

Travis felt a twinge of envy for what these two had together. He knew that Abby and Cade had had a rough time working through their pasts, and they deserved this happiness. But it was still hard to take as an outsider.

"How do you two get anything done?" Travis asked jokingly.

Abby grinned. "We organize our time." The couple shared a secret look. "We gave up arguing."

Cade glanced at Travis, then back to his wife. "I was in denial about my feelings for a long time. I don't know why. Joy is the best thing that ever happened to me."

Travis thought the same thing once. "I'm happy for you two, but love's not for everyone."

Cade grinned. "Just never say never, it will come back to bite you in the butt. Wouldn't hurt to take a second look at the pretty visitor upstairs. This time without a scowl on your face."

Travis had taken too many looks. "And you'll never open in the spring, if I don't get going on the Web site," he said, guiding the topic back to business. "Your ideas aren't going to go anywhere as long as they remain in this kitchen."

"Right," Abby said. "We need to get started advertising."

Cade looked at his wife. "It's your call, honey. Do you want to use Josie's pictures?"

"Oh, yes," she assured him. "They're perfect. So much so that I'm thinking that maybe later on, we could have Josie take some more pictures and frame the enlarged prints and then sell them in the gift shop."

"Jeez, there's a gift shop, too?"

Abby nodded. "One's planned for just off the highway. A general store and gift shop combination, but the building might not be finished by the time we open in April."

"You guys are going all out," Travis said.

"And we want you involved in it, too," Cade said. "Remember the Circle B is part yours. You already agreed to the cabin construction on your land. Later in the spring, they're going to start the work around the lake on Chance and Joy's property, the old Kirby Ranch. It's going to be a campground. With their land connected on the west side of the Circle B and our land…"

"Brandon's," Abby corrected. "My dad left the Moreau Ranch to Brandon."

Cade smiled. "With our son's land meeting up on the other side of the valley we're all together. So the Mustang Valley Guest Ranch includes a nature retreat, and by midsummer, a campground with swimming and fishing. And next year, Abby and I plan to turn Moreau Ranch into a working guest ranch. Well, I think we have about everything covered. Don't know what else people will want."

"Boy, you guys have been busy."

"I've told you about it," Cade said.

"Guess I've had my own thing going. I haven't been paying attention to anything else."

"Well, not any more," his brother said. "The family needs your expertise to help us pull off the opening of the Mustang Valley Guest Ranch."

Before Travis could answer, the sound of voices coming through the back door caused them to turn as Chance and his wife, Joy, walked in. The petite blonde had big blue eyes and a bright smile as she carried their baby daughter, Katie.

"Hey, the reinforcements are here." Cade stood and kissed Joy on the cheek and took the baby. Little Katie squealed in delight as her uncle raised her high in the air.

"Do we have to work Travis over to get him to agree, like we did when we were kids?" Chance asked teasingly.

It was Joy who came to the table and hugged Travis. "No, I think your brother needs to know that his family wants him to share in this venture." Her gaze was warm and loving. "It wouldn't be the same, Travis, if you weren't involved in this. I know how much Chance has wanted his brothers home."

Travis looked at Chance and Cade standing side by side. "It's true, bro," Cade began. "We've wanted to include you in this project. Say you'll work with us."

Travis hadn't been with his brothers in a long time. He found he'd missed it. And he wanted, needed, to return. "I don't know anything about running a guest ranch."

"You know about business," Cade said. "Besides, we're all learning. We're forming a corporation. Mustang Valley Inc. That way we'll protect all three of the ranches involved. Just the bordering sections of the properties will be included in the corporation. We don't want to threaten Chance's horse breeding business, or my son, Brandon's, inheritance from Abby's father. And I think we're all in agreement we want the Circle B to remain a cattle ranch.''

Travis glanced around the room and saw the eager looks. What else did he have to do? At least he could stay until he discovered what to do with his life. ''Okay, I guess you're stuck with me.''

The room broke into cheers, and his brothers wrapped him in a big hug. Then came his sisters-in-law. The room was loud with chatter when Travis noticed Josie standing in the dining room, silently watching the scene. He couldn't miss the sadness in her eyes. Something tugged at his heart, and he started toward her, but she was already making an exit.

He caught up with her at the doorway. ''Hey, don't leave.''

She paused, but didn't look at him. ''I didn't want to intrude on...family matters.''

Damn. He realized that she had just lost hers. ''You won't be intruding, besides, you know everybody.''

She shook her head. ''I'll just go back upstairs.''

Travis realized he didn't want her to go. He reached for her, and when he touched her she pulled away and started to lose her balance. He caught her and lifted the tiny woman in his arms.

''Put me down,'' she demanded.

''Not until you promise to stay off that ankle.''

''Who you got there, Trav?'' Chance came into the room, followed by the curious trio of Cade, Joy and Abby.

"Just a stubborn woman who doesn't know how to listen."

"Neither do you," Josie complained. "Now, put me down."

Travis didn't miss the glances exchanged between Joy and Abby, then Abby came forward. "Josie, I'm glad you're here," Abby began. "We wanted to tell you the job is yours. That is, if you want to stay."

Travis noticed Josie's questioning gaze. He knew she was waiting for his approval. Feeling her warm body against his and his heated reaction to her, he knew the best thing was to send her on her way. She was too tempting, and would only cause him trouble. But she was all alone, and he couldn't turn her away.

He looked at his family. "Of course Josie will take the job."

Chapter Four

Three days later, Josie sat on the bed in her bedroom, her hands trembling as she held the aged, yellowed piece of paper. The twenty-five-year-old letter Hank Barrett had sent to her mother was just one page. However, the short note said enough to crush Elissa Romero's world.

Dear Elissa,

   With a heavy heart, I write this letter. I'm a coward and can't face you to tell you what I must. Elissa, you have come to mean so much to me, and that is why I can't lead you on. There can never be a future for us. For one thing, I am much older than you are. It may not seem like a lot now, but twelve years is a big difference.

   Most importantly, I loved one woman, my Mae. Although she is gone, in my heart she is with me, and that wouldn't be fair to you. You deserve a man who loves you totally, and without ghosts from his past. I wish you all the happiness in the world.

Always,
Hank

Tears spilled down Josie's face, and she quickly wiped them away. In the few months she'd known about her father and his letter, she'd read it over and over again, hoping there would be something between the lines that would say that Hank Barrett had wanted Elissa Romero in his life. But he hadn't loved her. Which probably meant he wouldn't want her, either. The realization was nothing new to Josie. She'd dealt with rejection before. But all her life she'd dreamed about a father, a man who would love her, be proud of her. But now faced with the opportunity to claim him, she was too frightened to take the chance.

A knock on the bedroom door made Josie jump. She quickly folded the letter and put it in the drawer of the bedside table. "Come in," she called, expecting Ella.

Instead Travis walked into the room. Josie tried to act casual, but this man had a tendency to get a rise out of her. Dressed in faded jeans, a black T-shirt and cowboy boots, he walked assuredly toward the bed. "You okay?"

"Sure," she lied as she wiped away the last traces of tears. "Just one of those hormonal moments."

"You seem to have a lot of mood swings."

She wasn't going to let him get to her. Not this time. "You ever think you might be the cause?"

"Who, me? I'm just a good-natured cowboy trying to be helpful." He grinned and her heart tripped.

Josie quickly glanced away. "Is there a reason for

your visit, or are you just here to brighten up my day?''

"As a matter of fact, I just came from the body shop. Bart Harris Auto Repairs. He'll be giving you a call later.''

"Did he say if my car could be fixed?''

"He's pretty sure. If the insurance company is cooperative.''

Well, they had better be cooperative. She had to have a car. Even if hers didn't look like much, the engine was in good shape and the car was paid for. Now all she had to do was come up with the insurance deductible. Thank goodness she had her job.

"But if yours doesn't come through, I am sure our insurance company will work something out.''

"What does that mean?''

"It means you aren't going to be without a car.''

"How long before it can be fixed?''

"Don't worry, you can't drive yet. Besides, I can take you anywhere you need to go.''

Great. Just what she needed, a bossy, know-it-all cowboy escort. "I want to know when I have to come up with the deductible.''

"And I said our insurance will handle it. Now, when do you need to be at the doctor's?''

"Not until tomorrow afternoon. But I'd like to get some more film and a few personal items.''

"I can drive you into town.''

"I appreciate your offer, but Ella said she would take me.'' Thank goodness. The last thing Josie wanted was to have to hang around this man.

Travis shook his head. "Sorry, but you've been ditched for a cute six-month-old named Katie. Ella is baby-sitting all afternoon.''

"That's okay, it can wait until tomorrow."

"I said, I can take you."

Great, just great. Josie knew she would lose this battle. She stood up, careful of her heavily wrapped ankle. Her foot was covered by an orthopedic boot to protect the injury, which made it possible for her to walk. As she limped across the room, Travis watched her closely.

"As you can see, I can get around fine."

"I thought the doctor didn't want you walking on it."

"He said if I didn't overdo it, it was okay. So there isn't any reason for you to carry me around anymore."

He grinned and in a husky voice said, "And here I thought you were enjoying it. I know I was."

A warm tingle rushed down her spine. "Well, you'll have to get your kicks somewhere else."

She headed for the door, hoping Travis didn't see the effect he had on her. The last thing the man needed was a bigger ego.

"This isn't the way to the ranch," Josie said.

Travis had one hand on the steering wheel and the other resting against the back of the seat. "I thought we'd go out to the valley. They just finished surfacing the new road yesterday." He glanced at her. "Maybe you'd like to have a better look around."

"I'd like that." And since she had her camera with her, she might be able to take some pictures.

"I figured you've been itching to go back."

"I have. I have some ideas for the brochure. So far, I haven't been able to do anything about them. I'd like to try a few out today."

"Just don't go crazy. And whether you like it or not, if the terrain gets rough, I may have to carry you...."

When she started to object, he raised his hand. "It's that, or we go back to the ranch."

"Okay, you're the boss," she relented. "Is that what you want me to say?"

"That's enough for now." Smiling, he turned off the highway to a gravel road and the truck began to bounce. Josie grabbed the handle above the window and held on. Finally he maneuvered the truck to the end of the road behind three cabins, set back about a hundred yards from the creek. Climbing out, he came around to help Josie out.

"Stay put," he ordered, then reached inside for her camera bag. He took her hand and together they started down the slight slope.

Travis was amazed at the changes that had taken place just in the past week. The slightly hidden cabins were small, just two rooms. The wood-stained structures were adorned with porches that faced east, toward the valley and the most beautiful sunrises. It was late afternoon now, and the sun was filtering through the large trees overhead, making comfortable shade in the Indian summer heat.

"It's so beautiful here," Josie said as they inched their way to the creek. "You and your brothers were lucky kids."

Travis grinned when they came to the water. He sat down on a large rock as Josie looked around the area. "Oh, I don't know about that," he began. "When I was about nine, I wouldn't have agreed with you." He drew a breath, remembering the trouble with his father. "It's a little tough to grow up in West

Texas when your daddy has just been convicted of cattle rustling."

Josie turned toward him, and he saw that familiar look of sympathy. He hated it, especially from women. He definitely didn't want it from this particular woman. She started to speak, but he stopped her. "You don't need to say how sorry you are, I've heard that all my life."

She placed her hands on her hips. "It must get tough carrying that big chip around on your shoulder."

"I don't have a chip, I'm just stating facts."

"Oh, brother, you're waiting for someone to turn and walk away in shock, aren't you? Well, you're not getting that reaction from me. Nothing you say could shock me." She glanced around. "And it looks like you've had it pretty good lately. I refuse to give any sympathy to three boys who have people like Hank and Ella to love them. Come see me when you've lived with a man who reminds you every day that you're not his kid but expects your gratitude for the honor of having his name." Her eyes flared, her breathing labored. "Get out of my face, Randell." She stomped away.

Travis was too surprised to react, then realized she had just told him off. Suddenly the wind picked up and the rain began. He looked up in the sky to find the threatening clouds, then felt the big drops against his face. He stood and started after her. "Hey, wait."

"So you can continue your sob story? I've got more important things to do—"

She gasped as Travis scooped her up.

"What are you doing?"

"Trying to keep us dry," he said and hurried his

gait, heading toward one of the new cabins. They made it to the porch just as the sky really opened up. He set her down, but didn't seem to be able to release her, not when she was looking up at him with those big hazel eyes.

"We made it," he said. His breathing was labored as he glanced down at her cotton shirt and noticed the raindrops had spotted the thin material. "Ah... you don't look too wet."

"No, I'm fine."

The wind picked up, swirling her loose hair, and goose bumps rose on her bare arms. Worse, he could see her nipples pucker under her shirt. "You cold?"

She crossed her arms. "It's just the temperature dropped so quickly."

"Yeah, feels good. It's been too hot." He turned away from temptation and went to the cabin door. He tried the knob. Not surprisingly, it was locked. He peeked in the window and discovered the room was bare of any furnishings. "Too bad Cade and Abby haven't gotten the place finished yet." When he turned back, the rain was sheeting off the porch roof. He wondered how soon before it would let up. How long would he be trapped here with Josie? He glanced through the raindrops to the truck farther up the hill. "I should have brought the blanket."

"I'm fine," Josie said as she hobbled to the cabin wall and leaned against it, taking the weight off her ankle.

Travis went to her. "We might as well sit down." When he helped her, he realized she was trembling. "You're cold."

"Just a little. I'll be okay," she said as she sat on the porch floor.

He sat down beside her. "Now I don't want you to take this the wrong way, but this seems like our only solution." He put his arm around her and pulled her against him.

"What are you doing?"

"Trying to keep you warm."

"I told you I was fine."

"You're shivering. You only have on shorts and a T-shirt. If you don't want warmth for yourself, then think about your baby."

Josie was so frustrated, she wanted to scream. Why did she have to be stuck here with Travis? Why did she have to be attracted to him? A man who was off-limits. Her life was already a mess. Her biggest fear was looming overhead. The last thing Josie wanted was to turn out to be her mother. Alone with a child, and loving a man who could never return that love. She hugged herself tighter. How did everything get so complicated in such a short time? She glanced around and decided she was trapped here with the most bull-headed man in the world.

But Travis was right about one thing, she was cold and the sun would be setting in a few hours. She finally relented and leaned into his warmth, resting her head against his shoulder. Immediately his body heat seeped through her clothes to her skin. And it felt good. Maybe too good. What she didn't want to think about was what Travis was doing to her libido. So he was a good-looking man. Any woman would react, she tried to convince herself. She needed his warmth. It was survival, plain and simple.

His arm wrapped around her back, his hand rubbing against her sensitized skin. Unable to resist, she closed her eyes, and let the feeling take her away.

"This isn't so bad, is it?"

Josie only managed a small nod, then allowed herself to drift off.

Travis sat there with Josie's sweet body pressed against his side. She might be relaxed, but he couldn't say the same for himself. His body was letting him know how painful the closeness was. Why this woman? Why did he have to connect with someone who gave him so much grief? She had to be one of the most infuriating people he'd ever met. But after her outburst about her stepfather, he could understand her toughness.

He glanced down at her. She also had to be one of the most beautiful people he'd ever met. Her coal-black hair was soft as silk. Her luminous eyes were mirrors of contradictions. They showed her heat and fire, but also her pain. Josie Gutierrez might act like one tough lady, but underneath she was vulnerable and needy.

What was worse, Travis was drawn to her. Too much. They were too different to be compatible and he didn't need any involvement now. That didn't stop the intense feelings he got when she came near him. This was crazy. He had a pregnant woman in his arms. A woman whom he felt held something back, a secret maybe. And yet, he still could stop worrying about her and the child she carried. She was alone. How was she going to make it?

Josie shifted in his arms and her breasts moved against his chest. He bit back a groan as she settled into his embrace. In sleep, she looked so fragile. And for all her pretense, he knew she was no different than anyone else. She needed and wanted someone. Unable to resist, he leaned down and kissed the top of her head.

"Oh, Josie, are you going to complicate my life?"

She moaned, and the seductive sound made his body react. The rain had slowed, and they needed to get back. He nudged her. Josie made another sound, and her arm moved over his chest to his neck. Then she scooted closer, her face innocently turned up to his. When she murmured his name, he wasn't able to resist.

Travis lowered his head to hers, and when his lips tentatively touched hers, she drew in a sharp breath. The action set his heart pounding, and he couldn't hold back any longer. He dipped his head and covered her mouth in a searing kiss. Tugging her closer, he ached for the feel of her softness. And she seemed eager for the contact, too, her lips parting, allowing him inside to caress and taste her sweetness. His pulse raced, his blood hot with desire.

Then suddenly he pulled away. Damn! What was he doing? He couldn't take advantage of her. Besides, he didn't need this complication.

"Josie," he whispered. He nudged her gently, coaxing her from sleep. "Come on, darlin'. The rain has stopped."

Slowly she blinked open her confused green eyes. "What happened?" But without waiting for an answer, she pulled back. "What were you doing?" she asked indignantly.

Her surly attitude toward Travis returned. "Not as much as you'd like," he accused.

She adjusted her shirt. "In your dreams, cowboy."

He grinned. "No, Josie, in your dreams."

* * *

The entire family came for supper that evening. The conversation was lighthearted and funny, but Travis noticed that Josie kept her distance. In fact, she hadn't said a word to him since they left the cabin three hours earlier.

Abby looked at Josie. "I hear you went out to Mustang Valley today."

Travis watched as Josie's face reddened. "Yes, I was going to take some pictures, but it started raining."

"That was quite a downpour," Hank said as he passed the bowl of mashed potatoes to Ella. "Hear you had to take cover at one of the cabins."

"Just the porch," Josie said. "The cabins were locked."

Travis nearly groaned when he caught the looks exchanged between his brothers and their wives.

"Just what did you do to…occupy your time?" Cade asked.

Josie looked so flustered, Travis decided to help her out. "Josie took a nap," he said. "I think I bored her."

Joy turned to Josie. "Are you feeling okay?"

Josie nodded. "I'm just tried. I can't seem to make it through a day without wanting a nap."

"It's understandable," Joy said. "Just indulge yourself now, because after the baby comes you won't get much sleep."

"But I still have to work."

"You can take breaks," Joy said. "Nothing is more important than your health and that of your childs."

Seven-year-old Brandon was seated next to his grandfather. "Grampa Hank," he piped up.

"What, son?"

The dark-haired child smiled. "Mom said we're going to have a baby someday." The boy turned to his mother. "When are we, Mom?"

Abby blushed bright red, then she looked at her husband.

Cade took his wife's hand and smiled. "Come here, son," he said to Brandon.

The boy went and stood between his parents. "It looks like you're about to get your wish, Brandon. Your mom is going to have a baby," Cade said.

Brandon let out a whoop. "Oh, boy," he cheered. "I want a brother."

The room broke into laughter, then everybody hurried to congratulate the couple. Travis did, too, but not without a little envy. He'd never thought much about kids of his own. Even engaged to Lisa, he knew she hadn't planned to add children to their union. It hadn't mattered at the time, but now, as he watched his brothers with their loving mates, he felt a little envious. Everything was changing. Six months ago, he and his brothers were all bachelors. Now his brothers were fathers, and he was a minority. His gaze went to Josie. A lonely minority.

After dinner, the women went into the kitchen to talk babies. Hank, Chance and Cade decided to watch a baseball game on television. Restless, Travis walked outside to the patio. That's where he found Josie.

"My family can be overwhelming."

"I think your family is wonderful," she said. "I hope you know you're a lucky man."

He nodded. "I kid around a lot, but believe me, I know how great it was growing up here on the Circle B with Cade and Chance. Hank's been the dad we never had." He looked down and saw the tears in her eyes.

"You okay?"

She nodded. "I hate being weepy all the time."

"Just so long as I'm not the reason."

That made her smile.

"Tell me about your family," he said.

"There isn't any. It was just Mom and me."

"Earlier you mentioned a man," he said. "Was he your stepfather?"

She drew a breath. "I really don't want to talk about it." She started to walk away and Travis stopped her.

"Josie, about today. The kiss. I mean, it was out of line."

Her gaze darted away. "We can't let that happen again. We don't even get along most of the time."

He tried to laugh. "We didn't have any problem this afternoon."

She stiffened. "A gentleman wouldn't have taken advantage of the situation."

"Darlin', you make being a gentleman damn hard," he said, then marched off toward the house.

Josie watched Travis walk away. She was angry that she'd let the man get to her. And somehow, she had to stop reacting every time he came close. She flashed back to this afternoon and how safe she felt being in his arms, sharing his warmth. And when he kissed her, she'd thought she would melt there on the spot. Never, ever, had she been kissed like that. And the dangerous part was that she'd liked it.

She had to remember, she was here for a job, a job she needed. More importantly, she wanted to spend time with Hank. Get to know him a little before she had to leave. Then she would be able to tell her child about its grandfather.

"Josie…"

Josie swung around to find the man she'd just been thinking about. "Hello, Hank," she said. "I was just getting ready to turn in."

He stopped her. "Don't let me chase you off."

She shrugged. "Thought you would like some privacy."

"Oh, Josie girl, I love having people around, especially pretty ladies."

"Does your blarney usually work?" She found she was hungry for this man's attention. She was hungry just to look at him.

Hank grinned and led her to some patio chairs. "Looks like you found me out," he said. "I've lived in a house filled with boys for more than twenty years. Ella says she's the only one who can keep me in line."

"What about your wife?"

His smiled faded. "Mae should have complained more but she never did. I wasn't always the easiest person to live with, either. In the beginning there were times when I'd spend twenty-four hours in the saddle then come home and sleep for a few hours and then go back out. Ranching isn't an easy life. Between Texas heat, drought and bad weather, you never know what's going to happen." He smiled. "But I wouldn't live any other way."

"Do you have any regrets?"

He looked out over the pool as a breeze rustled through the trees. "You always have regrets. I regret that I didn't have Mae with me longer. She died before she even turned forty. I regret we never had children together.'' He studied her for a long time, then leaned forward and took her hands. "Does this have anything to do with your baby? Do you regret that new life inside you? Try to think of it as a gift, Josie. As for the man who left you, he should be whipped. But it's his loss."

She blinked, trying to hold back her emotions. "I love this baby.'' She touched her stomach protectively. "And she will always know that.''

"So this is a little filly you're carryin'?"

Josie smiled. "I'm not sure. I don't care, as long as the baby is healthy.''

"Then we'll make sure of that. As long as you decide to stay here, you will eat and rest properly.''

Josie knew her job here wouldn't take longer than a month at the most. She had to move on, make a home for her baby, find another job.

"I can't thank you enough for your hospitality, but as soon as I'm better I'm leaving.''

He nodded. "I understand. But just so you'll know, you're welcome here as long as you'd like.'' He squeezed her hand, then stood. "I think I better turn in.''

Josie had a hard time letting go of his hand. She wanted to hang on, to grasp some of the attention and love he showered on his family. But if Hank Barrett discovered who she was, would he want her in his life? Too afraid to find out, Josie decided she'd stay until she wore out her welcome.

Chapter Five

Two days later, Travis rode Rocky in from the southern section. Since sunrise, he'd been busy helping one of the hands, Ben, repair some downed fence, before moving one of the herds to another pasture. He was sweaty, tired and badly in need of a shower and some food.

As he headed toward the barn, Travis heard laughter and glanced over at the corral where Hank and two other ranch hands were gathered. He took a second look to see that Hank was dressed in new-looking jeans and wearing his new Resistol hat. In fact, all three men looked their Saturday night best as they stood against the white metal fence. Across the corral Josie was aiming her camera in their direction.

"Well, I'll be damned…I'm out here working my butt off, and these guys are standing around posing for pictures." He eyed the two hands, Jesse and Larry, local boys he'd known since high school. Back then the two couldn't do anything but act goofy around girls, and it seemed as if nothing had changed. Travis climbed down from his mount and wandered over.

"Come on, Hank," Josie said. "Smile like you want people to come to Mustang Valley."

"I don't want to scare them off," he commented. "You need to take a picture of someone a lot better-looking and a lot younger than me."

"You're plenty handsome," she told him.

The remark made Hank grin all the more, then he glanced toward the barn and noticed Travis. "Hey, son." Hank waved. "Come over here."

"Oh, no. I don't have time to get my picture taken," he snapped. "I've got better things to do." He looked at Josie and found she was examining him closely.

"You're perfect," she said as she limped toward him in a fitted pair of white shorts that hit about the middle of her trim thighs, revealing a shapely pair of legs. Her soft pink blouse was sleeveless with the tails knotted at her tiny waist. As usual, her long raven hair was braided and hung down her back, except for the few contrary curls around her face.

Realizing he was staring, he glanced away. "I'm filthy."

"And we're trying to sell a working ranch." She gave him the once-over again. He felt a surge of heat, and it wasn't from the Texas sun. "Women love the look of a man all sweaty and dirty from physical work." She made it sound almost sensual.

"I think you're crazy," he told her. "I'm going to shower." A cold one, he thought as he started to walk away, but stopped when he heard her murmur "Chicken."

He turned back and sent her a challenging glare. "What did you say?"

She shrugged. "Just wondering why you were so afraid of a little camera, or do you think that women will see your picture and come looking for you?"

He stiffened. "That's ridiculous."

"What's ridiculous? What I said about the camera, or the women?"

He put his hands on his hips. "I'm not afraid of either."

It was barely noticeable, but he saw her mouth twitch. "Okay, if you won't pose, I guess I'll have to use Jesse and Larry. At least they aren't afraid to give me what I want."

Travis looked at the two men who were grinning like fools. "You've got to be kidding. Those two can't stand straight and look intelligent at the same time."

She smiled. "They have been very cooperative."

"I just bet." He gave her another long look, knowing that she could probably sweet-talk a snake.

"You know what would be nice?" she asked. "If you would have a few pictures taken with Hank. This is a family ranch after all."

The woman fought dirty. "I don't have a problem with that. I just need to shower and shave first."

"No, you're perfect just the way you are. You have that authentic cowboy look." She took his hand and pulled him into the corral.

"So she managed to lasso you," Hank teased.

Travis wasn't going to admit to anything. For the next fifteen minutes, he let Josie tell him how and where to stand. She was quick and efficient. He appreciated that, until she came over and started manhandling him, tilting his hat or brushing back his hair. The feel of her hands on him was unsettling. Then, there was the scent of her. Nothing more than soap and her own freshness, but it was enough to set his pulse racing. Finally he'd had about all he could stand.

"I've got to go," he said.

Instead of arguing, she just nodded. "Thanks, Travis. I got some good shots. I hope we can do it again."

She'd caught him off guard. "Maybe you should pick on Chance and Cade next time."

"Good idea. I can use the three of you. You'd be great on the brochure. Real-life Texas cowboys. The ladies will love it."

Travis put his hands on his hips. "What are we selling here? I thought this place was for people who want to get away. Not women looking to hook up with a cowboy for the weekend." He turned and marched off toward the house. Darn woman. Why couldn't she just leave him alone?

"Travis," Hank called.

Travis stopped to let Hank catch up, but he really didn't want to rehash this over anymore.

"I know I was too harsh with her, but—"

Hank raised a hand. "That's right, you were. Josie's doing her job, and we all have to pitch in. A few pictures won't hurt you, and some encouraging words would be nice for Josie to hear."

Hank was right. "Okay, I'm sorry."

"It's not me you need to tell." He glanced over his shoulder, then walked to the house.

Ah, hell. Travis headed back to the corral, but Josie had left. He wandered into the barn, down the center aisle, and found her at one of the stalls. Standing on the bottom rail, she was petting the pregnant mare.

"Aren't you a beauty?" she crooned.

It was obvious she knew her way around horses, her way around a ranch and her way around his family. Was that what made him so angry? That she seemed to fit in too well?

"Sissy likes to be rubbed along her forehead, but be warned, once you start, she won't want you to stop."

Without looking at him, Josie's hand went to the white blaze on the chestnut face. "Well, let's give the lady what she wants. Us mothers-to-be should stick together."

Josie wanted to ignore Travis, but it was difficult. The man drew attention like a magnet, even filthy dirty and smelling of horses. She wished he would leave. "I thought you had to shower."

His stare made her look at him. "I do, but I wanted to apologize for the way I acted. I've been out working since dawn. I'm bone tired and plain out of shape." He chuckled. "I probably won't be able to get out of bed tomorrow, but that isn't any excuse for my behavior."

"Thank you," she said.

"You don't have to thank me, Josie." He took off his hat and ran his fingers through his sweat-damp hair. "I was out of line."

"I know." She forced herself to look at him, and all she could think about was the kiss they'd shared a few days ago. He'd been avoiding her ever since. "I know you don't like me being here." Travis was obviously uncomfortable with her accusation. But he didn't deny it.

He removed his hat and slapped it against his thigh. "It's not you personally," he said. "I'm just going through some rough times."

"And I came along and invaded your privacy. I'm not here to cause anyone any harm, Travis. And I'll be gone just as soon as my ankle is better and my car is fixed." She raised her gaze to his face. Even needing a shave and a good wash, he was still the best-looking man she'd ever seen. But things were way too complicated to add a man to her life. Josie needed to stay clear of Travis. She was here for Hank only, to spend some precious time with her father. What she had to be careful of was not to get her heart broken in the process.

Travis watched Josie with his family at the dinner table. Tonight, there were just the four of them seated at the kitchen table. Josie had taken over cooking the meal. She'd made pot roast that melted in your mouth, and Hank had been praising her efforts since his first bite.

"I think I've died and gone to heaven," Hank said. "This is delicious. I bet you and your mother had standing room only in your diner."

"We had a pretty steady business," Josie admitted.

"What's happened to the place since your mother's death?"

"My stepfather sold it." Travis saw a flash of sadness in her eyes before she ducked her head.

"That's a shame." A grin appeared on Hank's face. "But I'm happy I get the chance to sample your cooking."

Ella set a basket of rolls on the table. "You're

happy to sample everyone's cooking," she said. "I've never seen a man eat like you."

"I work hard, need to keep up my strength."

Ella made an unladylike grunt as she sat down. "You just like to stuff your face."

"Correction, I like *good* food."

From years of experience, Travis knew there was trouble brewing and he quickly changed the subject. "Josie, I was wondering if you have any suggestions on what pictures you think would work for the Web page?"

She looked confused by his question. "Some of Mustang Valley would be nice, and of course, some of the cabins. I need to develop the pictures from today, then I was thinking about taking some pictures at Cade and Abby's place."

"Sounds like a plan. And maybe you could come to the study later, I've been working on a logo."

"Sure."

Hank smiled. "It's nice to see that things are moving along so well. Before we know it, business will be booming."

Dinner was finished a short time later. Josie offered to clean up, but Ella sent her out of the kitchen, saying Hank would clean up. As Hank started to protest, Travis took Josie's hand and led her into the large study.

Josie stopped inside the door, and she gazed around the room. Honey-oak-paneled walls met the earth-tone carpeting under her feet. All the furniture was man-size, from the large desk to the floor-to-ceiling bookcases that were overflowing with books.

"It looks like someone likes to read," she remarked.

Travis nodded. "If it's a western, or a mystery, Hank probably has it here." He went to the crammed shelves. "He had us read every night, rain or shine, winter or summer. He told us life was a great teacher, but so were books. I don't think I ever met another man who is as knowledgeable as Hank, and he didn't get to finish high school."

Josie sat down on the overstuffed sofa and tried to absorb all the information about her father. There was so much she didn't know, and she hoped she'd have the time to learn more about him.

"Has Hank always been a rancher?" she asked.

Travis nodded. "He told us he's never gotten a paycheck for anything else. Says he can't think of another job he'd rather have."

Josie found herself envious of all the years the Randell boys had had with Hank. "You were lucky to have him."

Travis walked across the room and sat down beside her. "Yes, we were. Sometimes you don't even realize what you have until something happens...." His gaze met hers. "I've been away a lot of years. I didn't come home as often as I should have."

"Why didn't you? You and Hank got along, didn't you?"

"It wasn't Hank," he said. "It was shame. My brothers felt it, too." He drew a breath. "It was because of our father. He was sent to prison."

Josie hadn't heard that part of the story. "Oh, I'm sorry."

He shook his head. "I'm not. Jack Randell was low-down scum. A rustler. He got what he deserved, but his kids didn't. We were judged even though we never did anything wrong. Chance and Cade were teenagers, and they fought back by getting into trouble. Since our mother had died the year before and there weren't any relatives who would take us, we were separated and put into foster care.''

Josie gasped. ''How awful for you.''

''It was hell all right. Cade and Chance kept running away and coming to get me. Finally a judge, a friend of Hank's, convinced him to take us in. It hadn't been that long since his wife, Mae, had passed away when we came to live on the ranch. He promised he would be fair to us if we worked hard in school and on the ranch.''

Josie had to blink back the tears, seeing the love shining in Travis's dark eyes. ''I take it you and your brothers were good,'' she said.

''The best. We were too scared not to be. We didn't want to be separated again. I was only nine. All I had were my big brothers.'' Travis's gaze locked with hers, allowing her to see the vulnerability of that child. ''It seems I still need them.''

Josie's chest tightened with emotion. ''I don't think we ever outgrow our need for family.''

Travis leaned toward her, touched her cheek, her tears. ''I know you miss your mother,'' he said, his voice husky. ''It has to be rough on you, being pregnant and alone….''

Josie had felt alone most of her life. But hearing him say it touched her deeply. She had to move away from this man, from his kindness, but he was too addicting, and she was too needy. ''Yes, I miss her,'' she said, her voice tight.

Before she realized it, Travis had her wrapped in his protective arms, pulling her close. Unable to resist, she laid her head against his chest, listening to the intense beating of his heart, his warmth circling her like a blanket. It felt good, so good. Her hand moved across his chest, feeling his strength through his shirt. She needed this safe place. For once she wanted to know what it felt like to lean on someone. Closing her eyes she let herself pretend. It had been something she'd done a lot as a child. Whenever things got bad, she just shut out the world and all the bad things. She wanted to pretend now. Pretend that a man like Travis Randell would want her. That he would care for her and her baby, and she didn't have to fight the world on her own.

"Josie…"

She didn't want to answer, to break the spell. She only made a purring sound, snuggling deeper into his strength.

"Josie…" he whispered again.

She managed to raise her head and looked up at his handsome face, his deep-brown eyes, his inviting mouth. "Travis…"

Travis breathed a curse as he lowered his head, and his mouth closed over hers. His reaction was swift and strong. He wanted her. He kissed her like a starved man, feasting on her mouth. Although he knew he shouldn't let this happen, he couldn't seem to stop it. He couldn't let her go. Her lips opened with a throaty moan and he slipped inside, sliding his tongue over hers. He leaned back and angled her body against his. She made him want and ache for more.

The sudden sound of voices caused him to tear his mouth from hers. They were both gasping for breath. Josie looked stunned and embarrassed.

"Oh, God." She started to pull away, but Travis held on to her.

"Shh, it's okay, Josie. It's just Hank saying good-night."

He finally released her and watched as she scooted toward the edge of the sofa.

"I'm sorry. I shouldn't have let you do that."

Travis wanted to laugh. "Like we had a choice. Darlin' it's like lighting a torch when we get near one another."

She glared at him. But all he could see was her mouth, all swollen from his kiss, and he wanted her even more.

"Don't look at me like that, or you'll get more trouble."

Josie jumped to her feet. "This was a mistake."

He stood, too. "Maybe it was, maybe it wasn't, but like it or not, we're going to be working together."

She jammed her hands against her hips, pulling her white T-shirt tight across her full breasts. Damn the woman, she would make him crazy before the week was out. He quickly walked to the small desk against the wall where he had his laptop computer. Travis had brought it from Houston, one of the few things he managed to keep. He grabbed a chair and placed it next to his.

"Here, sit down," he told her.

As Josie took a seat, he could see how tired she looked. "I spent the afternoon playing around with some ideas. I wanted you to see some before I show them to Cade and Abby." He brought up the page as she leaned forward. The first thing that appeared was the silhouette of a Mustang and the name, Mustang Valley Guest Ranch.

Josie read aloud, "'A nature retreat for anyone who wants to enjoy a beautiful secluded valley where mustangs, along with many other types of wildlife, roam free. It's a perfect place for bird-watching, hiking and bike riding. Our cabins are nestled among the trees but have all the modern conveniences.

"'Not far away, for those of you who prefer the more authentic cowboy's life, we have the working section of the ranch. You will be able to ride along with the cowhands, and we'll show you how to drive the herd. Every spring and fall there's a roundup. You can stay in the bunkhouse, or in the privacy of your own cabins. Hope you'll come and spend some time enjoying the quiet ranch life of West Texas.'"

Travis rushed on. "It's still rough, but I needed to put something down, just to get an idea."

"It's great," she said. "I'm sure that Abby will want to add even more details. Especially about the honeymoon package she plans to offer."

"Of course," Travis agreed.

Travis could see that Josie was nervous about sitting so close to him. The last thing he wanted was for her to feel afraid of him. "Josie, stop acting like I'm going to pounce on you."

"I'm not," she denied.

"Look, I take full responsibility for the kiss."

"That's just it, Travis, you are *not* responsible, I am. I'm the one who kissed you."

A slow smile creased his mouth. "Well, ma'am, I was trying to be the gentleman, but if you insist..."

Josie groaned in frustration and smacked him on the arm. "Will you stop that."

"Stop what?"

"I'm trying to be serious here, and you're clowning around."

"And that's wrong?"

She glared. "It's wrong because we can't get involved. It would be crazy. With my situation..." Her voice softened. "I mean, I'll be gone, and you're going to be happy about that."

"Yeah, happy. You and the baby are going to be out there on you own, trying to make a go of it, God knows where."

She jumped up. "Travis, you're not responsible for me or for my baby."

She was right, but why did he feel differently? "What kind of life will you have with a tiny baby and no job?"

"I'll be fine, really."

He studied her for a long time, then finally said, "Who are you trying to convince, Josie? Me or you?"

Chapter Six

The next morning, Josie walked out of the doctor's office. After a complete examination, he deemed her ankle had healed nicely but ordered her to take it easy for a week or so. Otherwise, she and the baby were in perfect health, and he scheduled another appointment for her in a month.

Was she going to be around then? Should she rent an apartment in San Angelo? What about when her photography job ended? The questions were reeling in her head. The only definite thing she knew was the time had come for her to move out of the ranch house. But to where?

Outside in the waiting room, she found Travis seated on the sofa, leafing through a magazine. Dressed in jeans and a western shirt, he should have looked like everyone else, but not this man. His presence drew attention. Besides his good looks and great build, Travis Randell had charm, and he could use it when he wanted to. But Josie wasn't taken in.

Okay, so his killer smile had gotten to her a few times, but she also knew the man's bossy nature. Like earlier when she asked him to wait in the truck, and he insisted he had to come in with her. And as if it were any of his business, he would probably have fifty questions for her.

Travis glanced up to see her. Tossing the magazine down he stood and walked over. He smiled and Josie felt her heart rate increase.

"What did the doctor say?" he asked.

Josie headed toward the door. "What I thought he'd say. That I'm fine."

Travis held the door and ushered her out into the bright sunlight. "How about your morning sickness?"

Who was this man, her keeper? "I didn't say anything because it's normal to be sick during the first trimester."

"Is that what the doctor said?"

She blew out a breath. "No, because I didn't waste his time asking him something I already knew. Now stop with the questions."

He raised his hands. "Okay, but I still don't think it's normal," he murmured as he helped her into the truck, then walked around to the other side and got in.

He handed Josie a gold-and-white envelope from the photo store. "While you were with the doctor, I went and picked these up."

"Oh, thanks," she said surprised. "You didn't have to do that."

He gripped the steeling wheel and sighed. "I know, but I thought it would save us some time. I wanted to run by Abby and Cade's this morning."

Josie smiled. "I'd like that." She'd wanted to see Abby again. "But I'm not sure I have anything to show them."

"Take a look," Travis said, nodding to the pictures. "If they don't suit you, we can go back to the valley."

She opened the envelope and started going through the photos she'd taken of Hank and Travis in the corral. Her chest tightened when she saw the handsome older man. He stood straight, his shoulders squared as he smiled at the camera. No wonder her mother had lost her heart to this rancher.

Josie continued to the next photos. The ones of Larry and Jesse. She smiled at the two cowboys hamming it up. Then she came to Travis's picture. She felt her mouth go dry as she studied his cocky stance, his fitted jeans covered by dusty chaps and a shirt that covered a muscular chest and broad shoulders. Her attention went to his face, the stubborn set of his chiseled jaw, the hat tugged low, nearly hiding those mesmerizing bedroom eyes. Oh, yeah, this man was definitely going in the brochure.

The temperature in the truck seemed to have risen. She went to the next packet of pictures—the trip to Mustang Valley when they'd gotten caught in the rain. She bit back a groan, remembering they had done more than just take pictures. Josie tried pushing aside the memory of their kiss. She could say she was half asleep and didn't know what she was doing. If that was so, what had been her excuse for kissing Travis again last night?

That was another reason why she should leave the Circle B. Travis was creating feelings in her that were dangerous. Dangerous for her because she would be the one to get hurt. She had to concentrate on getting her life settled. She needed a home. Spring would come soon and so would her baby. "Can I have a look?" Travis asked.

She glanced across the truck to the handsome man. The sooner she left the better. She handed them over and watched his deadpan expression as he went through each photo.

"How did you get the sunlight to do that?" He pointed to the picture of the valley where the sun had bright streams of light rays shooting down to the valley.

"I used a special filter over the lens. It creates a nice effect, doesn't it?"

"Almost mystical."

"Thanks. It really wasn't that hard. I took some classes and learned a few tricks."

He continued to go through the rest of the pictures. "They're all good, except the ones you took of Larry and Jesse in the corral."

"What about the ones I took of you?" Josie asked.

He tossed her a sexy grin. "It's not my opinion that matters. But if you want authentic, I guess you got yourself a working cowboy."

She'd gotten a lot more. Travis's picture oozed sex appeal. "I bet Abby will like the one with you and Hank, too."

He laughed. "Abby would think that Cade is more appealing."

Cade was good-looking, too. But hands down, Travis knew how to use his charm. "I guess it's a matter of taste."

He gave her a sideways glance. "Why, I didn't think you noticed, darlin'."

She started to open her mouth to deny it, but what was the use? "Boy, it's sure getting crowded in here with that huge ego of yours." She busied herself putting away the pictures. "Didn't you say we were going out to Cade and Abby's place?"

Still grinning, Travis reached for his cell phone and made a quick call as they headed out of the parking lot. After getting an invitation to stop by, they were on their way.

Fifteen minutes later, Travis turned off the highway and drove under the gate that read Moreau Ranch. A large two-story house came into view. The sparkling white shutters and trim were proof the place had been recently painted. The outer buildings, including a large barn, had also been freshly painted.

Travis helped Josie out of the truck. "It's quite a place, isn't it?"

All Josie could do was nod as she grabbed her camera bag.

"This place belonged to Abby's family," Travis began. "Tom Moreau had one of the biggest spreads in the area, but it fell on hard times. That's the reason Abby and Cade are turning the place into a working guest ranch, so they won't have to rely on the cattle business for their livelihood."

Suddenly Josie was worried about Hank. "Does— does the Circle B have trouble, too?"

Travis shook his head. "No, Hank has always been into other things, and he lived a more conservative life than old Tom did. And Hank owns his land outright. You can't say that about a lot of other ranchers."

They walked across the gravel drive toward the

barn. "What will happen if this guest ranch doesn't work out for Abby and Cade?" Josie asked.

Travis smiled. "I don't think they'll go hungry. Cade was a financial planner for years before he came home and married Abby." His hand rested on Josie's waist as he ushered her through the doors and into the large building. The cool air felt good against her heated skin, all except for where Travis was touching her. And he didn't seem to be in a big hurry to let her go.

Voices from down the aisle drew them to a stall where Abby, Cade and Brandon were admiring a new colt. All three turned and gave greetings, Josie couldn't resist and pulled out her camera.

"Do you mind?" she asked.

"Shoot away," Cade said.

Travis couldn't help but watch as Josie moved around and snapped several shots of the two-day-old foal. In her jean skirt, pink T-shirt and tennis shoes, she was a graceful picture herself. She danced around the stall trying for the best photo op. She wasn't even limping. He wanted to warn her to be careful with her ankle, but knew he had no right. She had as much as told him, several times. Another smile lit up Josie's face as she coaxed Brandon to turn a certain way. Travis wished she'd favor him with one of those smiles.

"A picture of the new foal will go great in the brochure," Josie told Abby. "People love babies." She continued to snap pictures, even luring Cade into posing, cowboy hat and all.

"That's it, cowboy, smile for the camera," Josie teased with too much of a seductive tone.

Cade blushed and Travis bit the inside of his mouth to keep quiet.

"I hope our guests never discover I'm better at the stock market than the beef market," Cade said.

Abby went up to her husband. "I remember you used to be a pretty good rodeo cowboy."

He laughed. "That was a long time ago."

Brandon interjected, "Dad gave me all his buckles."

"That's great," Josie said. "You'll have to show them to me sometime."

The boy beamed at the dark-haired beauty. Another one bites the dust, Travis thought as Brandon and Josie wandered off for more pictures of ranch life and a picture of his horse, Smoky.

Ten minutes later, they returned, Brandon still talking a mile a minute.

"When I get older, I'm going to have lots of horses like Uncle Chance. He has my grandpa's horse, Dancer. And he's going to breed him so I can make a lot of money."

Everyone laughed. Cade ruffled Brandon's hair. "That's my son. Always looking at things from the money angle."

"I think it's time we went inside," Abby said. "Brandon, why don't you run ahead and tell Carmen that Travis and Josie will be staying for lunch." She looked at the two. "Please, stay. We'd like to discuss some business, and I'm dying to see the pictures you've taken."

"That's fine with me," Josie said and looked at Travis.

"I'd like some of Carmen's cooking."

Abby smacked her brother-in-law. "You have no

problem eating anyone's cooking." She then turned to Josie. "I hope you're not overdoing it. How's the ankle?"

"I'm fine. In fact, the doctor gave me a clean bill of health this morning."

"Good, but you still have a baby to think about."

"That's what I've told her," Travis added.

Josie sent him a frown, then smiled at Abby. "What about you? You're having a baby, too."

A blush appeared on Abby's face as she touched her stomach. "Oh, I'm taking it easy. This big guy stops me from doing too much."

Cade came up behind her and wrapped his arms around her middle. "That's right. I'll be shadowing her for the next seven and a half months."

Abby leaned into her husband. "Oh, I think I'm going to like all the attention."

At the loving sight, Travis felt a pang of envy. He couldn't help but wonder if he would ever be able to feel that way about a woman. He was still stinging from Lisa. He looked toward Josie. What about her? Did she still love the baby's father? He tensed. How could she when the man deserted her?

"Well, I don't know about you guys," Abby said, "but I'm going to take Josie into the house where it's cooler."

"We'll be in in a few minutes," Cade promised as he leaned down and placed a kiss on Abby's lips. "I just want to show Travis the bunkhouse."

"You mean the hotel?" Abby smiled as she glanced at Josie. "What started out to be just some remodeling of the old bunkhouse for guests has turned into a huge job."

"We want our guests to be comfortable," the older Randell brother said.

"I'm surprised you haven't suggested room service," Abby said as she and Josie walked from the barn.

Cade was still grinning when the women disappeared, then he sighed. "Ain't love grand?"

Travis glared. "When did you start acting so sappy?"

"Oh, man, the right woman will do that to you."

"Well, all I've found are the wrong ones. So, I'm sorry if I don't share your enthusiasm."

"What about the looks you were giving Josie?" Cade asked as they walked out back of the barn to the long white bunkhouse.

Travis had never been able to hide much from his brother. "I'm just worried she's overdoing it. I mean, I feel responsible."

"For what?"

He sighed. "I caused her accident."

"You weren't driving."

"No, but since I found her that morning with a camera, I warned her I'd be watching her and she'd better not try anything." He rubbed his hand over his face. "I thought she was a reporter from Houston, trying to get a story."

Cade shook his head. "You're about as bad as I was. When it comes to trust, we Randells are a sorry bunch. I'm just glad that Abby was patient enough to wait until I admitted I loved her."

Travis waved his arm. "No, I'm not falling into any relationship. Not after Lisa. And especially with a woman who already has her own baggage." Not to mention he still suspected she was hiding something.

"Are you talking about Josie's baby? Are you saying you couldn't love a child unless it was yours?"

"No, I didn't say that," Travis said. "If anything, that kid is the innocent one. I'm just not going to put my heart on the chopping block again."

Cade shook his head. "Oh, then you're going to miss it all."

"Miss what?"

"Miss all that good lovin' when the right woman comes along."

"I told you I'm not looking for love."

Cade laughed. "Famous Randell last words."

Josie envied Abby's life. A nice home, a loving husband. Their baby was going to be so lucky to have two loving parents. "This is a beautiful place. Later, I'd like to take some pictures."

"Sure, anytime. Cade and I have put in a lot of work recently. I'd like to show it off." They walked up the steps to the porch. Abby held the door open, allowing Josie into a mudroom, then a large kitchen where a heavyset woman was at the stove. Her hair was pulled back into a bun at the base of her head. Her features and dark color showed her Mexican heritage.

"Josie, this is Carmen. Carmen, Josie."

With a bright smile, the housekeeper greeted her with, "*Buenos días,* Josie."

"*Buenos días,* Carmen," Josie answered.

"No need to hurry with lunch, Carmen, just call when you're ready. We'll be working in the study."

"Too much work. You need to eat, the baby needs nourishment."

"I'm eating plenty," Abby said as she pulled Josie

along with her. "Maybe I should have kept the baby a secret awhile longer. Everyone wants to feed me."

"You're lucky to have so many people who care about you," Josie said as they walked into the large room.

The eggshell-colored walls were a nice contrast to the dark hunter-green carpet. The honey-brown leather sofa faced a slump-stone fireplace. An oak desk was placed in front of French doors that led to a patio. There was another table along the wall, set up with a computer, printer and all the latest high-tech electronics.

That was where Abby headed. "I know I'm fortunate. My first pregnancy was a lot different."

Josie was confused and Abby saw it.

"Brandon is Cade's child, but we weren't together then. My father decided he knew what was best for me, and a Randell wasn't good enough for his daughter." A sad look washed over Abby's face. "Anyway, because of my father's threats to hurt Cade, I ended up sending him away and marrying another man."

Josie knew that she wasn't doing a very good job of hiding her shock. "I'm sorry, I didn't know."

"It's not a secret," Abby said. "But I was lucky, Cade came back into my life again. We had to overcome a lot of problems, but our love won out and Brandon has his father."

Abby sat down at the desk. "I've never been happier. Cade and I have a great life. And it's going to get a lot better when we get Mustang Valley Guest Ranch off the ground." She smiled. "Now, can I see the pictures?"

"Sure," Josie said and pulled the envelope from her bag.

Abby looked at each as she laid them out on the desk. "Oh, Josie these are good."

"I know you wanted morning shots, but the only time I've been able to get out to the valley was the other afternoon."

Abby pursed her lips. "I may have been wrong, I like this one with the sunlight filtering through the trees." She continued to study the photos. "Which ones do you like?"

"Well, this one," Josie said. "It shows the creek and the valley. I'd like to go back when the mustangs are there, unless you want to use the shots of the horses I took that first morning."

"I think we can use both." Abby sorted through more pictures. "Oh, I love these shots of Hank and Travis. They're priceless."

"I'd like to take some of Cade. Do you think he would pose for me around here? We need real cowboys to sell the idea of a working ranch."

"You mean by 'real cowboys' some good-looking men to bring women with cowboy fantasies to the ranch?"

"I guess that's what I'm saying."

"No need to sound worried. I know my husband is good-looking. In fact, all the Randell brothers are handsome." She winked. "But I'm sure you noticed that."

Josie turned away. What was she supposed to do, lie and say Travis was ugly? "It's hard not to."

"Well, then, let's sell it, and make sure we hire a lot of single attractive ranch hands."

They were both laughing when the men walked in. "What's so funny?" Cade asked.

"Oh, nothing. We're just talking about the ranch."

Cade looked concerned. "I'm wondering now, with the baby and all, if this project's going to be too much."

"We didn't plan this baby at the most convenient time," Abby said.

He took his wife in his arms, his eyes sending a private message. "As far as I'm concerned, we planned everything perfectly. And I'm going to be here with you." His hand touched his wife's stomach, and Josie wondered what it would be like to have someone love her like that.

Her gaze went to Travis, and she was surprised to see him watching her. Another jolt of awareness shot through her as she felt heat move to her face.

Finally Cade drew everyone's attention. "Now, let's go have lunch. I'm starved." He put his arm around his wife's waist and together they walked out. Travis came to Josie. "Sorry, they kind of overdo the happy couple stuff. You'll get used to it."

"It's great. It's the way love is supposed to be."

"Too bad it's not like that for all of us."

Three days later, it was midmorning when Josie finally awoke. She'd gotten up before dawn yesterday, and Hank had taken her out to the valley. She wanted to get some more pictures of the mustangs. She smiled, remembering the coffee and the sweet rolls he'd brought along so she wouldn't get hungry.

But today was another day. Josie knew she could hold off what she had to do. Leave. Somehow she had to tell Hank, and delaying it wasn't going to change things. He'd been kind enough to allow her to stay this long. She slowly sat up, wanting to see how her stomach was going to act. When the wave of nausea didn't come, Josie still wasn't going to test fate. Just for a precaution, she picked up the stack of soda crackers from the nightstand, took one and began nibbling. So far so good. She took another bite, then another. After two crackers, she deemed her stomach fine.

She stood and began gathering clean clothes for her shower. She went to the connecting bathroom and opened the door. A gasp escaped her lips when she found an intruder. Travis was standing at the sink shaving. Her gaze moved down his bare chest to the towel wrapped around his waist.

"Oh, I'm sorry. I had no idea you were here. I figured you'd be gone. It's so late...." No rambling, she ordered herself.

He acted as if this were a common thing. "I was out this morning, moving Rufus. That damn bull and I had a little disagreement." He rinsed off his razor, then turned and faced her, allowing Josie to see the purplish bruise along his rib cage.

"Oh, Travis. What happened?" She rushed to him.

Travis sucked in a breath as her hands touched his bare skin. She'd taken him by surprise. And the last thing he wanted was to see her looking all tousled and sexy from sleep. Not when he knew every night she'd been sleeping only a few feet away. He closed his eyes as her fingertips moved over his tender flesh. Boy, her hands were lethal.

"You should see a doctor."

She tilted her head and looked up at him. Her greenish-colored eyes sparkled. Darn, she was so beautiful. "What you're doing feels pretty good."

To his surprise, she didn't remove her hands.

"Travis, you've got to get an X ray. The bull could have broken a rib."

He shook his head. "I've been thrown off a few horses and had broken ribs. This is just a painful bruise. But if you want, I'll let you nurse me."

This time she did step back. "I don't think you need me."

He slipped her hand in his, and eased her into his arms. "Oh, darlin', you couldn't begin to know how much I need you."

Josie gasped. "Travis we agreed we weren't going to do this." She pushed at him, and he immediately let her go, causing her to stumble backward. The movement made Travis's towel come loose, but before the terry cloth slipped away, he grabbed it.

Josie's eyes widened over the near mishap. "I'm sorry I disturbed you. It won't happen again since I'm leaving today." With those words she swung around and walked out.

It took Travis ten minutes to dress. His sore ribs slowed him up considerably. But he wasn't going to let Josie just walk out. Was she crazy? She had no place to go. She didn't know anyone around here, and she couldn't go back to El Paso. He walked downstairs and found her in the kitchen sitting at the table with Hank.

"Are you sure there isn't anything I can do to talk you into staying a spell longer?" Hank asked her.

Silently, Travis walked in and went to the coffeepot and poured himself a cup.

He watched as Josie smiled. "I hadn't planned on staying this long. Hank, you've been more than generous."

"Just taking care of my responsibilities," Hank said. "You were hurt on my property."

Travis leaned against the counter. "Where are you headed—without a car?"

Her gaze shot to him. "It should be fixed, any day now."

Travis shrugged and that action pulled at his ribs. "That's what the body shop told me last week. But who knows?"

Josie glanced at Hank. "I can't keep taking... I mean it's been nearly two weeks."

"You know, Josie," Hank began, "I think I may have a solution to your problem. Since you need to be close by to take the pictures, why can't you stay?"

"But—"

Hank raised his hand. "Wait a minute. Not here at the house, but in one of the cabins."

Travis tensed. "But there's nothing out there. There's not any furniture."

Hank noted Travis's concern. "There were some deliveries yesterday. I know for sure the beds came. Now, it may be sparse for a while, but we can supply you with some linens and stock the shelves with food."

"What about electricity?" Travis added.

Again, Hank looked up. "We had that turned on when you had those security lights put in." He looked back at Josie. "You'd be helping us out, too. We need to work out some of the kinks in the place. If you agree to stay then we'll know what to do to make our guests more comfortable."

Travis was beginning to like the idea. The valley wasn't exactly close to the house, but it was better than Josie running off to God knows where.

Hank grinned. "What do you think, Josie? You want to stay? We'd sure love to have you."

Travis saw the tears in her eyes. "How can you turn that down?" Hank said.

"It's such a generous offer I can't," Josie answered.

Hank grinned. "Good," he said and stood. "I'm going to call Abby and see what needs to be done yet."

Travis watched him walk out, then turned to Josie. "I guess you'll be staying after all." He may be sorry, but he was glad she wasn't leaving.

Josie's gaze met his. "How do you feel about it?"

He shrugged. "Doesn't affect me one way or the other."

Her hazel eyes bore into his. It was as if she could see something. "You're not very trusting are you?"

Travis slowly shook his head. "No, not anymore. I've learned my lessons the hard way."

"And now everyone else has to pay because a woman did you wrong."

He frowned. "Who said it was a woman?"

Josie stood and folded her arms across her chest. "If it was another guy, you'd just duke it out with him and move on. It's a woman all right."

He tensed. "Stay out of my personal life."

She ignored him. "Look, Travis, I'm sorry that you loved someone and she hurt you, but it wasn't my fault. And I'm tired of taking the blame. I need to stay here to finish this job, but after that I'll leave and be out of your hair for good." Then she swung around and marched out of the kitchen, leaving him to brood on his own. Damn. Why couldn't he just let it go? Josie was right, she'd be gone soon enough.

All he needed to do was stay away from her. Far away.

He closed his eyes and recalled what happened just moments ago upstairs…the feel of her hands on him, the tenderness of her touch. He drew a sharp breath as his body came to life. He wasn't going to survive the next few weeks. Somehow he had to figure out a way to stay clear of Mustang Valley and one Josie Gutierrez. That was if he knew what was good for him.

Chapter Seven

Josie rolled over in bed and read the digital numbers on the clock. Seven o'clock. Smiling, she looked up at the beamed ceiling overhead and inhaled the scent of newly cut wood. It had taken an extra day, but thanks to Abby and Cade, she was moved into the cabin.

Josie scooted up, leaned against the headboard and glanced around the spacious room. A used-brick fireplace was the central focus of the room. Terra-cotta tile covered the floors and earth-tone braided rugs added warmth. An overstuffed sofa and matching chairs were grouped around a cedar chest. A round maple table and four chairs filled the space in front of a huge window adorned with wooden blinds, the slats tilted so thin sheets of sunlight invaded the cabin. The kitchen area was small but equipped with all the modern conveniences.

The queen-size bed she'd slept in last night sat in an alcove along with a dresser and a small closet.

Another door led into a small bathroom tiled in almond and blue.

Josie sighed. She was going to love staying here in this haven of peace and quiet. Just her and baby. She touched her stomach knowing it was too soon to feel any movement, but she wanted to make a connection with the new life inside her. "We're going to be fine. I just need a little time to think—to plan our future. But I promise you, baby, I will always be here to take care of you."

A loud pounding on the door startled her. "Josie, it's me, Travis," he shouted. "We need to talk."

She groaned. "So much for peace and quiet." She climbed out of bed and grabbed her robe. Pulling it over her short gown, she hurried across the room and opened the door.

Travis Randell stood there in his usual western shirt, worn jeans and a scowl. Her stomach tightened, and she had to fight the sudden queasiness. "Good morning, Travis."

He ignored her greeting and paced the small porch. "You were right."

This was a first. "Right about what?" she asked.

"It was a woman. Her name was Lisa, and we were engaged to be married. But I'll have you know that she not only two-timed me with my business partner, but she ran off with him and my money and destroyed my good name to boot. So you can see why I'm a little bitter." His eyes narrowed as he studied her. "You okay? You look pale."

Travis didn't get an answer. Josie shot off to the bathroom. He heard the door slam, then he heard the sound of her retching. Damn. He thought she was over that. He charged inside and marched to the bath-room and rapped on the door. "Josie, you okay?"

"Go away," she called weakly. Then he heard her getting sick again.

Concerned, he pushed open the door to find her leaning over the toilet. He darted across the small area and used his arm to brace her limp body as she emptied her stomach. Then he took a cool washcloth and pressed it against her flushed face. Silently, he gave her a glass of water to wash out her mouth, then lifted her and carried her back to bed.

"I don't need to be in bed," she argued.

"Shh, I'll decide that. You're as weak as a new calf. Just rest." He went into the kitchenette and turned on the teapot. After finding some peppermint tea, he pulled down two cups and filled them with hot water. Then he located her soda crackers. Carrying a tray, he went back into the bedroom. She appeared to be sound asleep.

He eyed her closely. She looked so tiny curled up on the big bed. Her long hair was spread in raven waves across the white pillow. His attention was caught by the rise and fall of her breasts, and his body tightened. He cursed under his breath for having wicked thoughts.

"Go away and let me die," Josie mumbled.

"I brought you some tea and crackers. Thought they might help." He set the small tray down on the bedside table. He picked up a cracker and held it in front of her face. "Take a couple of nibbles. It'll help."

She opened one eye. "How do you know?"

"Abby told me."

Grudgingly, she grabbed the cracker from him and took a tiny bite, then another.

"Good," he said, then picked up her tea, and crouched down beside the bed. "Here, have a little of this."

Her gaze was suspicious. "This something Abby told you, too?"

"No, Ella used to give us tea when we had an upset stomach." He smiled when she took a sip. "Feelin' better?"

"A little, but I usually do after I've emptied my stomach."

He picked up his cup, sat on the floor and leaned against the dresser. He took a swallow, hoping the brew would calm him, but the fact was, he was worried about Josie. "I thought you were past this."

She remained silent.

"Have you talked to the doctor about you being sick all the time?"

"I'm not sick all the time. And no, I haven't said anything because morning sickness is normal for pregnant women. I'm only two months along. This could go on for a while. I'm sorry I messed up your day." She placed her cup on the table and rolled over.

Go away, she screamed silently. The man was infuriating. Why did he always have to be around when she was at her lowest?

"Josie, I'm not going anywhere," he said. She felt his weight on the mattress, his hand on her shoulder. "What I'm going to do is call the doctor and check."

The man was driving her crazy. She rolled back over and caught a flash of tenderness in his compelling brown eyes. Her mouth went dry. "Fine."

"Then if you're up to it, I thought you could help me decide on pictures for the Web site."

"I'd like that."

"That's only if the doctor gives his okay."

She nodded, knowing it was useless to argue with him.

Smiling he stood and pulled a small cell phone from his shirt pocket, then punched out the numbers for information. He got through, but the doctor was with a patient and would call him back.

Josie didn't want to wait around. "I'm going to take a shower." She sat up and Travis reached for her. "Don't even think about asking if I need help."

There was that grin again. "Why, darlin', I was just concerned. But remember I'll be right out here in case you need me."

Josie gathered her clothes. "I'm perfectly able to wash myself."

Travis leaned against the dresser and folded his arms. "Oh, but it's so much fun when you share the experience."

Heat shot up Josie's neck to her face as she hurried into the bathroom, hearing Travis's laughter even after she shut the door. The man made her crazy. Why couldn't he leave her alone? A better question might be, why was he being so nice her? Before he'd always wanted her gone, but now he was hanging around.

Josie reached into the shower and turned on the water. She took off her robe and gown and stood in front of the mirror. Turning sideways, she examined her flat stomach. She wasn't showing yet, but soon she would be. Then a man like Travis Randell would run away fast. And that was for the best. Her baby was going to be wanted and loved. A tear ran down Josie's cheek. She was going to make sure of that.

Travis watched as Josie climbed around the rocky edge of the creek and bit back a warning. She'd already threatened to banish him back to the ranch house if he made any noise. She wanted to capture the mustangs undisturbed.

He knew she was right. After his conversation with the doctor, he realized Josie was fine and that he had to stop being so protective. The wisest thing to do was to get in his truck, head back to the ranch and never return. But he couldn't. Something kept pulling him toward her. He couldn't leave her alone.

Josie's Nikon dangled from around her neck as she made her way back from the creek. "Oh, they're beautiful. The buckskin stallion especially." Her smile was wide, lighting up her eyes. "I can't believe you've had this place all to yourselves."

Travis managed to tear his gaze away from her and look around. "Yeah, we were pretty lucky," he said. "For the longest time this was our escape. Whenever we had a problem, we'd ride out here. This place was where we felt we belonged, alone with all the other misfits."

Her eyes met his. "That morning you found me, you were here trying to work out some things."

He shrugged. "I guess. But for my problems, I don't think even the valley has the answers."

"I'm sorry," she said. "I'm sorry about Lisa. I'm sorry you lost your business."

"I can't believe I dumped all that on you." He didn't want her pity.

"I guess we just bring out the best in each other," she said as fine strands of hair blew across her face.

"Yeah, but I always did like setting off a firecracker." He leaned closer, tempting himself with her pouty mouth, knowing that if he did kiss her they'd both ignite in flames.

"Sometimes it's easier to talk with strangers."

"Still, I didn't need to spill my guts." He removed his hat and combed his fingers through his hair. "I just wanted you to know, my anger wasn't meant for you. At least it wasn't supposed to be."

"Is there anything that can be done?"

"I've got someone working on straightening out the mess with my business."

"What about Lisa?"

"I stopped feeling anything for her a long time ago," he told her, finally admitting it out loud.

Josie's gaze locked with his. "It hurts to be betrayed."

Was that what had happened to her? "How about you? How do you feel about your baby's father? You still love him?"

She stiffened and pulled back. "No. I don't love him. I never loved him. So, what does that make me?" She glared at him, then turned and started up the slope at a hurried pace.

Travis went after her. "Josie, wait," he called, but she didn't stop. At the cabin, she went inside and tried to close the door, but he came inside anyway.

"Go away," she ordered as she removed her camera and set it on the table.

"I'm not going anywhere. If you think I'm judging you, you're wrong. I only asked because I thought you might still be carrying a torch for this guy."

She sat down and blinked back the threatening tears, then shook her head. "I was with my mother when she died. There was no one else...I was alone. I was scared...I needed someone—another person to tell me things would be all right again." The tears spilled over on her cheek and she brushed them away. "Frank...Frank Hobbs and I had dated, but until that night we never...I never..."

Josie didn't struggle when Travis drew her into his arms. She began to sob into his shirt as he silently held her, so close he wanted to absorb her into his skin. To share her pain, to help heal her. "Your baby was conceived that night," he breathed.

She nodded, then looked up at him. "I don't regret what happened. I want this baby, and I love her."

He smiled. "I have no doubt you do. Are you sure it's a girl?"

He thought she was going to hit him, then despite herself, she smiled. "Yes. A sweet baby girl." Her hand touched her stomach.

A strange thing happened to Travis. His hand moved to cover hers. They shared something special, private. The act seemed innocent, yet so intimate without being sexual. "A sweet baby girl it is," he whispered as his gaze locked with hers. "Just like her mother."

"I am sweet. You just bring out the worst in me."

"Let's see if I can find some of that sweetness." He dipped his head and tasted her lips. She sucked in a sharp breath, but didn't pull away. He lowered his head again. This time, he took teasing nibbles along her bottom lip. "Mmm...you taste good, but I have a feeling there's more." His mouth found hers, he parted her lips and pushed his tongue inside to duel with hers.

Josie knew it was insane, but she couldn't seem to help herself as she wrapped her arms around his neck and pressed closer to his body. It felt too good to connect with another human. But this was a risky game and someone could get hurt.

"This isn't a good idea," she said, but made no move to distance herself.

"You're telling me. But I think maybe I found a way to stop our fighting."

"Maybe we should quit while we're ahead."

"Where's your sense of adventure?" he asked, as his mouth returned to hers for another heart-stopping kiss.

Josie was lost in Travis's arms, the strength and comfort of his embrace. She didn't want to think beyond how wonderful he made her feel. But soon common sense won out, and she called a halt to the craziness and broke away. "Whoa, cowboy, I think things are getting out of hand," she said a little breathlessly.

Travis smiled against her mouth. "And this is a bad thing?"

"Yes. We've both been hurt by past relationships."

"So, what's wrong with being friends...being friendly?"

She gave him her best incredulous look.

"Don't you see," he continued, "you and I. We have no secrets."

Josie fought hard not to look guilty, knowing Travis had a knack for reading her too easily. How would he react if he discovered her relationship to Hank? At this point, she didn't want to know. She liked the temporary peace between them. She wasn't foolish enough to think anything serious could happen between them. A few laughs and some kisses shared with a good-looking man. As long as she remembered that one day…soon, she would have to pack up and walk away.

Problem was, could she handle that?

Three days later, Josie walked into the Circle B's kitchen carrying a large dish of homemade enchiladas. She wanted to thank everyone for all the help they'd given her and told Ella she was bringing dinner.

"Food's here," she called, drawing Ella's and Hank's attention.

Hank grinned and got up from the table to greet her. "Well, lookie here what Josie brought us." He took the dish and set it on the table. He turned back and hugged her. "We've missed you, Josie girl," he told her.

"I've missed everyone, too," she said, meaning every word. She hadn't seen Hank in three days. She treasured every one of his touches and hugs, knowing that in a few weeks she'd be finished with the photos. In fact, she'd been looking for work around town.

Ella smiled. "Hi, Josie."

"Hi, Ella," Josie greeted, then looked over her shoulder to see Travis coming into the room. Her heart began to race as their eyes met.

His dark eyes swept over her approvingly. "Josie, good to see you."

"Good to see you, too," she said, but in truth Travis had been a frequent visitor at the cabin. He'd tell her that they needed to work. He brought his laptop computer, but a lot of the time, they'd ended up going for a walk. They'd hike for hours around the valley, Josie with her camera, taking pictures. More than a few of the shots were of the handsome Travis Randell.

"Look, son, Josie made us enchiladas," Hank said. "My favorite."

"It's been a while since I've made them," Josie said. "I'm not sure how good they are."

Travis crossed in front of her on his way to the coffeepot. "Oh, I think anything you cook would taste good," he said, then leaned forward and murmured, "Like you do."

Heat shot to Josie's cheeks as she turned away. "I guess we better get this in the oven if you want to eat anytime soon."

"I've already preheated the oven," Ella said, then opened the door and allowed Josie to slip the casserole inside.

"About thirty minutes," Josie said. "Ella, do you want me to help with the salad?"

"No, everything is ready. Why don't we visit for a while? Seems like forever since you've been here."

"It's just been a few days."

"So how are things at the cabin?" Hank sat down at the table with his coffee. "Are you lonely?"

Josie refused to look at Travis, but she could feel his gaze on her. "A little, but I've been busy taking pictures." She reached into her purse and pulled out a piece of paper. "Before I forget here's some things that Abby wanted me to check out in the cabin. Some of my ideas for improvements." She found it difficult to concentrate on what she was saying under Travis's close scrutiny. She finally turned her attention to him.

Dressed in a freshly laundered tan shirt and jeans, he had his arms crossed over his chest and smiled as if he knew a secret.

Hank's voice drew her back. "How is it since the phone was installed? I was worried about you out there alone."

"It's great. I'm sure the guests will be happy that they can call the ranch for emergencies."

"And your car. Is it running okay since you got it back?"

"Better than ever. But I need to pay you the deductible the insurance company didn't cover."

"That's between you and Travis," Hank said. "He picked up the car."

She looked at Travis. "Don't worry about it," he said. "I made a deal with Bart at the shop."

"What kind of deal?" she asked. Not only had her car been fixed, but surprisingly, the car had a new coat of bright-red paint. She had a feeling that Travis paid extra for that.

Hank laughed. "Knowing Bart, he probably made you promise not to enter any events at the Circle B Rodeo."

Travis never took his dark gaze from Josie's face. "That was for the paint job. For the deductible I have to talk him up to Mattie Lewis at the rodeo."

Both Ella and Hank broke into laughter. "That sounds like Bart," Hank said and looked at Josie. "He's been after Mattie for the last three years. She's divorced and sour on men. But Bart swears she's the only woman for him."

"You could have warned me," Travis said. "Now, I've got to spend the day playing cupid."

"Hey, we've all done it," Ella said. "Every time

I take my car in, Bart cuts me a break on the charges, then gives me little messages to give to Mattie at choir practice."

Hank looked disappointed. "Trav, you have no time to play matchmaker. I have you signed up for the bronc riding competition. Chance and Cade are signed up, too." The older man grinned. "You three are going to win all around."

"What rodeo?" Josie asked.

Travis shrugged. "Just a small rodeo the Circle B puts on for the neighboring ranchers. The only people who can enter have to work on a ranch in the area. It's the last weekend of October."

"It's a lot of fun," Hank said. "The women cook all the food and the men put on the entertainment."

"You mean you men act like fools," Ella corrected. "If you decide to ride a bronc this year, Hank Barrett, I'm going to visit my sister until you heal, which will take six months."

"I only did last year because I was goaded into it," he said. "But I have to enter something. People will think I'm getting old."

"You're still the best roper around here," Travis said.

Josie would like to see Hank in action. "Maybe you could divide into age groups?" When everyone looked at her, she explained. "Age groups, like senior, junior and juvenile."

Travis and Hank exchanged a glance. "Might not be a bad idea," Travis said. "Then it would even out the competition."

"You may have something, Josie," Hank said. "I'll talk it over with some of the other ranchers." He smiled. "I know one thing, if those enchiladas taste as good as they smell, you better bring them to the rodeo.''

"I'd love to.''

Ella took plates down from the cupboard and began to set the table. Josie got up to help her, pretending not to notice Travis's stare, but she had to admit, she liked his attention. Any woman would find it hard to ignore a man like Travis Randell.

About ten o'clock, Josie was back at the cabin, but she was too restless to sleep. She went out to the porch and sat in the lawn chair and looked up at the full moon. Never in her life had she felt so at home. So at peace, as if she belonged here.

She didn't. This was just a peek at the life she could have had if her parents had gotten together. If Hank Barrett had loved her mother. But he hadn't. And this wasn't her home. Tears welled in her eyes. Angry with her weepiness, Josie blinked them away and started to go inside when she heard something. She listened again, first hearing only crickets, then the sound came again. A horse's hooves against the ground. She looked out as the moonlight illuminated the rise, and saw a horse and rider coming toward her. Travis. Her heart raced as he tugged on the reins to stop his horse by the other side of the porch.

"Travis, what are you doing here?''

"I came to see you.''

"But you just saw me.''

The animal shifted, breathing hard through his nostrils. Travis leaned against the saddle horn. "Too many people. Want to go for a ride?''

Josie was thrilled at the idea but... "I shouldn't. The baby.''

"I wouldn't let anything happen to you. Besides, Rocky is gentle as a lamb." He slid backward off the saddle, then held out a hand. "Come on, I'll even give you the best seat."

Josie didn't hesitate. "How can I turn that down?" She gave him her hand, put her foot in the stirrup, and he pulled her up. With a slightly awkward ascent, she finally made it, then Travis took control of the reins and turned the horse toward the creek. Josie leaned back against Travis's warmth and let the lazy rocking of the horse lull her.

"I haven't done this in years," he said.

"Take a girl for a ride?" she asked, realizing she was jealous.

"No, ride at night. I tried once to take a girl, Jody Benson, but Hank caught us. He said it was too dark to see where we were going and suggested we come inside and watch some television instead." He sighed. "That definitely wasn't how I'd planned to spend the evening with the prettiest girl in the senior class."

"And just what had you planned?" she asked, wishing she had known the young Travis.

"Why, Ms. Gutierrez, a gentleman never kisses and tells."

"I guess I'll just have to use my imagination."

"Go ahead, but the truth was, nothing ever happened. And I never got the chance to bring another girl out to Mustang Valley. And rightly so, my brothers and I had made a pact. This was our private place." He laughed. "I found out recently that Cade broke the promise when he brought Abby here. In fact, their son Brandon was conceived here."

Josie didn't say anything as she listened to the story.

"It was the only place they could meet because Abby's father didn't want his daughter to be with a Randell."

Josie felt him tense. "I'm sure not everyone felt that way."

"Enough did to make our lives difficult."

Josie looked up at Travis. "I wouldn't have felt that way," she said.

Rocky stopped and Travis cupped Josie's face with his hand. "Oh, darlin' if I'd known you in high school, I think I would have forgotten about everything else, including my determination to go to college."

She swallowed back the dryness in her throat. "I doubt it. I was pretty skinny in school. My mother called me a late bloomer."

In the moonlight she could see his grin. "Well, all I can say is you made up for lost time," he said. "You look perfect now." His head lowered and his mouth captured hers.

Josie didn't resist as his lips caressed hers until she ached for more. She turned as much as possible until she was nearly lying in his arms. He broke off the kiss.

"Damn, what you do to me." He went back for more kisses, each one growing more and more intense. His hand moved to her blouse and cupped her breast through the fabric. Josie gasped and Travis used the opportunity to slide his tongue inside her mouth, hungrily tasting and stroking.

A coyote cried in the stillness and Josie pulled away. "Travis, we can't do this."

Travis didn't want to hear her rejection. Not when he'd been aching for her every night since they'd met.

"You don't want me to stop, Josie." As if to prove it, he unbuttoned her blouse, then pushed his hand inside her bra and touched her already puckered nipple. He drew a sharp breath, then shifted her body so he could lower his head to taste her.

"Oh, Travis," she cried as he drew the bud into his mouth and suckled, giving them both pleasure. He still wanted more, much more. He wanted all of her.

"Let's go back to the cabin," he said.

Cradling Josie against him, Travis managed to turned Rocky around. Within five minutes, they arrived at their destination. Travis got down, then lifted Josie in his arms and carried her inside. He didn't stop until they were in the alcove. Then he placed her on the bed and sat down beside her. Her blouse gaped open. He released the clasp on her bra, and her breasts burst free.

"You're so beautiful," he proclaimed, then he lowered his head and took her mouth in a heated kiss. He stretched out beside her, pulling her against him. This time his hand covered her breast, brushing his fingers across her pouty nipple. She whimpered in pleasure. "Josie, I want you. Let me make love to you."

She stiffened, then tried to push him away, but he wouldn't let her go. "Josie? What's wrong?"

"I can't," she cried. "Please, Travis, I can't...I can't."

"Shh, it's okay." It really wasn't, but he wouldn't push her. "I'm not going to do anything you don't want me to." He saw her tears. "Please, don't cry."

"I didn't mean to lead you on," she whispered, and pulled her blouse together.

"It doesn't take much." He forced a laugh. "You

can just look at me....'' She did, and desire shot through him, but it was more. Feelings he didn't understand or even want to define. All he knew was he wanted to hold her, to take care of her. How much he looked forward to seeing her smile.

Oh, God. What was wrong with him? He closed his eyes, drawing a needed breath as he sat up on the edge of the bed. And even though Josie might expect it, he couldn't walk away from her. He cared too much.

He turned toward her and took her hand. ''If things were different... I mean, I can't offer you anything.''

Josie didn't say a word. Then after a while, she took her hand back and said. ''Look, I think it would be a good idea if you leave.'' He didn't miss the sadness in her voice. ''We both have made enough mistakes.''

Travis wanted to argue that their being together didn't feel like a mistake, but she looked so fragile. ''Okay, I'll leave, but I will be back, Josie.''

He got up and marched out the door. He climbed on Rocky, then dug his heels into the horse's sides and took off. The cool air felt good against his skin, but it didn't erase what he was feeling or what nearly happened with Josie.

She had him so confused. He knew one thing—he sure as hell needed to get his life straightened out.

Chapter Eight

Around midnight, Travis walked from the barn toward the house. Rocky had been brushed thoroughly after the hard ride and settled down for the night. But the roan wasn't the only one who'd needed to unwind. Travis had spent the last hour trying to push Josie from his mind. It would be the only way he'd get any sleep tonight.

But his thoughts kept returning to the scene at the cabin, and the beautiful and willing woman in his arms. A woman who, for the short time she'd been here, had driven away all his common sense. Even worse, she'd managed to steal her way into his heart.

Travis stepped into the kitchen where a single light glowed over the sink. He swore he wasn't going to let another woman get under his skin. Once burned, twice shy. He should have learned to keep away from fire. But after tonight, with sexy Josie Gutierrez so close and the taste of her sweet kisses, he wasn't so sure. He wanted her, so badly every cell in his body ached.

Thank God Josie had had the sense to send him away. But the crisp air on the ride home did nothing to cool his jets. He still wanted her. And he had no right. Besides his share in the Circle B, he had nothing. No business, no job prospects, nothing. What could he offer her?

Whoa. Travis paused realizing the direction his thoughts were taking. Was he actually thinking about a future with her...and her baby? Lord, was he crazy? Josie didn't want anything to do with him.

He headed toward the stairs and noticed a light coming from the study. Just as he was about to check on it, the door opened and Hank walked out into the hall.

"Travis," he called.

"Hank. What are you doing up this late? Something wrong?"

"No, just waitin' on you." He smiled. "And I wanted to pass on some good news. The private investigator, Rucker, called after you left. It seems he located Lisa and Byron, and the police have them in custody."

"Well, I'll be dammed!" He found himself grinning.

Hank handed him a piece of paper. "Your lawyer, Matthew Hayes, wants you to call him. He needs you to fly to Houston and sign some papers. I'm not sure of all the details."

"I'll call Matt." He glanced at his watch. It was nearly midnight. "Guess I better wait until morning." He looked at Hank. "Sorry if I kept you up. You could have taped the note to my door."

"Didn't mind at all," Hank said. "It's been a while since I've waited up for any of you boys. How was your ride?"

Travis nodded. "Good. Nice night and Rocky likes to run."

"You like to run, too," Hank said. "How's Josie?"

Travis's heart nearly stopped. "How did you know I rode out to see her?"

Hank smiled. "You couldn't take your eyes off her all through dinner. Of course that's nothing new. Since you two met, you've either been mooning around her like a lovesick calf, or snapping at her like a stallion at a teasing rail."

Heat suffused Travis's face as he opened his mouth to deny it. But the look on Hank's face told him that it was useless. "Okay, I'll admit I'm attracted to her," he conceded. Then he added, "but that doesn't mean we're right for each other, or that I'm going to do anything about it." He had already gotten more involved than he'd meant to.

Hank raised an eyebrow. "If you say so."

"C'mon, Hank. You know I just got out of a mess with Lisa. My business is in the toilet."

The older man nodded at the note in Travis's hand. "Looks like things might be getting straightened out."

Travis didn't want to let himself hope. "But Josie...she's had a bad experience with her baby's father. She doesn't need me...."

Hank held up his hand. "You can make up all kinds of excuses, Travis. But from my experience the only thing that counts is how you feel in here." He pointed to Travis's chest, his heart. "Once a woman

gets in your heart, it's hard to get her out." A sad
smile touched his weathered face as if he were remembering his Mae. "But you have to figure that out
for yourself. I hope your trip to Houston goes well,
and that you get back in time for the rodeo. I want
my boys to make a good showing this year."

"You want us to make you proud," Travis said.

Love showed in Hank's soft hazel eyes as he said,
"You've already done that a thousand times over,
son." Then he wrapped Travis in a tight embrace and
whispered, "I want you to be proud of yourself."

Since about six in the morning on the day of the
rodeo, Josie had been busy helping the ladies in the
kitchen prepare food. She'd never seen so much potato salad in her life, even when she worked at the
diner. Kept on ice for later was anything from hot
dogs to top sirloin steaks for the grill.

Dozens of people had been arriving since early
morning. She peered though the yellow gingham cur-
tains framing the window to see the results of the
men's work. Three sets of portable bleachers had been
carried out from the storage shed and set up at the
corral. Rows of picnic tables lined the tree-shaded
areas decorated in an autumn theme for the festivities,
and tons of food waited to be served to the hundred
plus men, women and children who were expected at
the Circle B Rodeo.

There was so much to do Josie didn't have time to
think about Travis not being around. She had no time
to think about the kisses that drove her wild, or the
way he caressed her, setting her skin aflame, or how
much she wanted to surrender to his lovemaking.

Nevertheless, it had been *all* she'd thought about

for the past three days. Ever since the night at the cabin when she'd asked him to leave.

She'd known for a while now that she was hopelessly in love with Travis Randell. And that was disastrous. The worst thing that could have happened. As crazy as the idea was, she couldn't stop dreaming about a future for them. Impossible, she told herself, especially when all this time, she hadn't been honest with him. How would he feel if he discovered she was Hank's daughter? She knew all too well what would happen. She'd been through rejection before. A sick feeling hit the pit of her stomach and worked its way up to tighten her throat. No, she couldn't go through that again. She would stay the stranger, and for a little while longer bask in the illusion that they all cared about her. She couldn't risk Travis finding out who she was—she couldn't let anyone find out. It was the only way. So why did her decision make her heart feel like it had just been trampled?

"Josie," Abby called her back from her reverie.

Josie glanced toward the back door. "What?"

"Hank's about to start things." The redhead took Josie's hand and they started out the door. Josie grabbed her hat from the rack, and they walked outside as groups of people began to mingle around the barn. At the corral there were colorful vinyl banners strung around the arena, waving in the soft breeze. Several pens were filled with rough stock for the day's events, bronc riding, steer wrestling and calf roping. Abby started up the bleachers, and Josie followed her. Near the top they took their seats next to Joy. Josie felt excitement rush through her. She'd been looking forward to today. It had been all Hank talked about the past week.

She glanced down at her ink-black Wranglers and smiled. They were a little tight, but she'd wanted to get into the rodeo spirit. She had on her best western blouse. It was a bright pink with black piping along the yoke. Her long hair was pulled back and adorned with a pink scarf, and Abby had given her a black cowboy hat to complete the cowgirl look.

The crowd stilled as Hank stepped up on the wooden bandstand across the arena, raised the microphone to his mouth and spoke. "Welcome friends and neighbors to the twentieth annual Circle B Rodeo." A round of applause and cheers broke out. "I'd especially like to welcome back two of my sons who have been gone for a while, Cade and Travis. And we also have some new additions to the Circle B family this year. Abby, Chance's bride and Joy, Cade's bride and their son, Brandon." Abby, Joy and Brandon stood and waved to the cheering crowd. Josie swallowed back her envy, wishing she could be counted as one of Hank's family.

"Now let's get this rodeo started," Hank announced and the crowd enthusiastically agreed.

Abby turned to Josie. "I'm excited, but scared. Cade's entered the bronc riding event this year."

Josie knew this rodeo had never had a bull riding event because of the danger, but that didn't mean the other events were completely safe. Hank had told her that the rodeo's rough stock came from local ranches and some from Chance's ranch. "I don't think you have to worry. I mean, Cade grew up on a ranch, he knows how to handle horses."

Abby didn't look convinced. "And for the past eight years he's been sitting behind a desk in Chicago. I just wish he'd stick to calf roping. Of course the

Randell brothers are entered in all events. Cade and Travis are partners for the team calf roping.''

''But Travis isn't here.''

Abby smiled knowingly. ''Oh, he will be,'' she said. ''He called this morning to let Cade know he was on his way.''

Josie's pulse took off. Travis was coming home. No sooner had the thought registered in her head than she began searching the crowd and turning toward the house. A tall, lean cowboy walked toward the grandstand in a loose-hipped gait that made her breath catch. Recognition was instant as she focused on the man in question. Travis.

From his coal-black Stetson that sat low on his head, to his silver buckle glistening in the sun, he was impressive. Her gaze eagerly moved over him. He wore new jeans covered with low-riding leather chaps. A starched teal-blue shirt hugged his wide shoulders and muscular chest, then tapered perfectly into a narrow waist.

Oh, God. No man had a right to possess such body-tingling sensuality.

She couldn't swallow as his deep-set unwavering gaze picked her out of the large crowd. Gracefully, he made his way up the bleachers, then stopped in front of her. The people all around her turned to watch as he leaned down and placed a tender kiss on her surprised mouth. She gasped as warmth ran through her.

''I've missed you,'' he whispered. His dark eyes were smoldering. ''Did you miss me, darlin'?''

Oh, boy, she was in trouble. Josie could only nod.

''Good, we need to talk…later,'' he said with a wink. ''I have an important question to ask you. But, now, I need to ride a horse. And I need a little help from you." He reached out and tugged the scarf from her hair, causing a shiver to run down her spine. "For good luck," he said, then tied it around his neck.

Before she could speak, the announcer came to the microphone. "All entries for the bronc-riding event report to the pens immediately."

"Better go," he said. He leaned toward her and took another kiss, then turned and made his way down. Josie couldn't take her eyes off him until he disappeared behind the bleachers.

"Whoa, maybe we should call for the water wagon and wet you two down," Abby said.

Josie blushed and glanced at the curious stares from the women in the stands. "I didn't even know he was home...."

"Well, baby-brother Randell has definitely returned, and if I'm not mistaken he's staking his claim...on you."

Josie felt panic and happiness surge through her at the same time. "No...he's just playing up the day."

"I doubt it, I know that look." She gave her a sideways glance. "Just relax and enjoy it."

Josie knew she wouldn't enjoy anything. Travis wasn't for her. She was leaving as soon as she finished the photos for the brochure. She had to, before things got too complicated. But Josie had a feeling things already were.

Travis made his way to the chute. His heart was racing, not only because he was climbing onto rough stock for the first time in eight years, but because all he could think about was Josie.

The three days in Houston had been hell. A legal

mess, but thanks to his sharp lawyer things hadn't turned out too bad. He'd even handled the worst part, coming face-to-face with Lisa and Byron. Actually, it hadn't been as hard as he'd thought it would be. It had taken him only seconds to realize his feelings for Lisa had died. In fact, he wondered if he'd ever really loved her. He knew that she sure as hell didn't love him. When he revealed his decision to prosecute, Lisa began to plead with him, reminding him of what they'd had together. All he could think about was getting home to Josie.

Travis heard the crowd cheer as Russ Talbert, one of the hands from the Rocking M rode out the eight seconds.

Now it was his turn. His brother, Chance, pinned his number on his shirt. "So, I hear you got a woman up in the bleachers cheering for you," he said.

"I just thought it would even things up since you and Cade have Joy and Abby."

Chance's eyebrow raised. "So this is serious?"

"That's up to Josie," Travis replied as he walked to the pen railing.

"Cowboy up," the chute boss called as Travis climbed up and over the top rung. His heart raced as he looked to the stands, then down at the buckskin horse, Slammin' Sammy. He swallowed hard. So he drew the toughest mount in the event.

He glanced at his brother. "It's only eight seconds," Travis called, remembering that's what they used to tell each other when they were kids.

"Go get 'em, bro," Chance yelled as he gave him the thumbs-up sign.

With a sturdy tug, Travis checked the leather strap with his resin-covered glove hand, then he swung his leg over the bronc. The nervous animal kicked out in irritation. Travis took another breath, trying to calm himself. It would be embarrassing if he passed out before he even got out of the gate. Again Travis started to set himself as the animal stilled for a moment, but he knew it was going to be short-lived. He braced his legs firmly on the rung of the chute and slid his gloved hand under the handle of the rigging, then sat down on the horse.

"Ready?" the boss called.

"Ready," Travis answered as the gate swung open, and Sammy charged out in a wild state. The body-jarring bucks were unbelievable, but somehow Travis managed to hold on, even pick up a rhythm. It wasn't the prettiest ride, but hell, he was hanging on. Then finally the buzzer sounded. Travis relaxed, but too soon. Before the pickup man could get to him, Sammy bucked him high in the air. The last thing Travis remembered was a collective gasp from the crowd. And the image of Josie's sweet smile. He hoped he could see it one more time.

Heart racing, Josie rushed from the stands to the arena. Travis lay facedown in the dirt. She had to get to him.

Josie wasn't the first to arrive. Already, medical technicians were there, but she managed to squeeze in and kneel down beside the still body. She took his hand. "Travis," she gasped. "Oh, God, Travis. Are you hurt?"

Slowly, he opened his eyes and blinked. Then came his wicked smile. "Promise not to leave me, if I said no?" he asked.

Heat warmed Josie's face. "Travis Randell, you scared me...us to death. I thought you were hurt."

"I am bruised a bit," he complained and motioned to his chest. "Will you kiss it and make it better?" He tried to raise his head but both the attendants and Josie made him lie back down.

"I'm fine. I didn't even lose consciousness. Just knocked the wind out of me. Did you see me? I stayed on the eight seconds."

"Yes, I saw you. I also saw you fall."

The attendants sat him up. "Take it slow," one of them ordered.

Travis nodded, then looked back to Josie. "I admit that wasn't too pretty, but I was on Slammin' Sammy. He's the meanest piece of horseflesh around here." His grin only got wider.

She'd had enough. "What is it with you men? You're not happy unless you scare the living daylights out of us."

"I didn't do it on purpose." Travis got to his feet, was handed his hat, then signaled to the crowd he was okay. When Josie started off, he reached for her and put his arm about her shoulders. "I need you with me," he said and together they walked out of the corral as a score of 79 was posted. The people cheered louder.

His brothers and Hank appeared. "You okay?" Cade asked.

"Yeah, fine. The wind was just knocked out of me."

Josie tried to step away, but Travis held on to her. Several other people came up and congratulated him on his ride. He thanked them and kept on walking with Josie. The rodeo continued on behind them as he led her into the barn. They went down the aisle until they reached an empty stall. He maneuvered her inside, into a dark corner. Josie's pulse roared in her ears as he pulled her close. Suddenly she lost the desire to fight or run away.

"Oh, you feel good. I've been aching to hold you in my arms since I got home. But just for the record, you're not going to push me away again, not unless you can convince me that we don't belong together."

Josie looked up at his sexy bedroom eyes, his chiseled jaw and stubborn chin. She was lost. She couldn't let him go, not yet. "I can't."

He grinned as he pulled off her hat. "That's all I need to know." His mouth swooped down and captured hers in a heated kiss. One of need and desire, one that had Josie's knees weak and her brain unable to think of anything but how much she wanted this man. How much she would always want him.

He broke off the kiss. "Damn, I missed you. Couldn't think of anything else but you. And believe me, I needed a clear head to think things out. But there you were, Josie," he said, then his mouth returned to hers and he rewarded her with a toe-curling kiss.

"I missed you, too," she admitted.

He pushed his hat back, allowing his brown hair to fall to his forehead. "I'm sorry about the other night, darlin'. I pushed you too far, and you weren't ready." His fingers traced her cheek. "You take all the time you need to think, but just so you know, I want there to be an us. I think you want that, too. I know you care about me, and I care about you. I couldn't say anything before because my life was in chaos...." He stopped his rambling. "I'm talking like a damn fool. Maybe Sammy did knock a few brain cells loose."

She touched his face. "You're doing just fine."

His eyes pierced hers. "So you're saying there's a chance?"

She couldn't admit that. Not yet. "Travis there are so many reasons—"

Someone called Travis's name from the barn entrance.

"Damn, I've got to get back. I promised Cade I'd partner with him in calf roping." He grinned as he placed his hat on her head. "You want to come and watch me make a fool of myself?"

"Are you sure you're feeling up to competing?"

"You made me all better. Really, I'm fine." He kissed her again. "I think I feel so good, I may just win all the events." His voice lowered as his gaze moved over her. "For you." His mouth met hers again. "We'll have to continue this later, darlin'." He took her hand and they left the stall.

Josie never knew she could be so happy and so unhappy at the same time. She couldn't lead Travis on. Somehow she had to find the strength to convince him that their relationship wasn't a good idea. But still reeling from his kisses, she would explain it to him…later.

Hank was a happy man.

The Circle B Rodeo couldn't have turned out any better. From the weather to the attendance, it had been the best in years, and when the awards were given out, the Randell brothers had been winners in all three main events. Chance took steer wrestling, Cade, calf roping and Travis, bronc riding.

Even Hank had placed in the senior calf roping event, but he didn't care about that. He was too busy bragging about his boys. He was also proud of his new daughters-in-law and the grandkids. People were probably sick of hearing about Brandon and Katie.

Now, he only had to wait for Josie and Travis to get together. The sparks had been flying between them since she arrived at the ranch, but Travis had been fighting it. After today, Hank doubted that boy could deny his feelings any longer. Not with that silly grin he'd been totin' around all morning.

Hank wished he could help them out. But outside of keeping Josie close by at the cabin, he knew he had to just stand back and let nature run its course. He believed that love would win out.

A neighbor, Gary Brown, came up to him. "Hank, when are you gonna get this party started? I'm mighty thirsty."

"I'm at it right now." Hank walked to the shaded area roped off for the barbecue. "Is everyone ready to party?"

In answer, he got cheers, and he jerked the tarps off the washtubs filled with ice and long-neck bottles of beer. The dry-throated cowboys started a line to quench their thirst. Over the twenty years of the rodeo, Hank had never allowed any alcohol consumption, even by the spectators, until all the events were finished. The last thing he wanted was any unnecessary accidents.

He walked to the barbecue pits and made sure they were fired up and manned. Steaks, hot dogs and chicken were already sizzling on the grates. The ladies were coming out from the kitchen, carrying side dishes. Several families had already staked their claims on tables. A bunch of kids, romping in the swimming pool, couldn't care less about eating. Hank sighed as he glanced around and caught sight of Chance, Cade and Travis laughing together. Joy and Abby stood nearby with the grandkids. Hank paused to enjoy the moment.

Life didn't get much better than this.

Chapter Nine

Several friends and neighbors stopped Travis to congratulate him on his win. He was polite, but he wanted to find Josie. He hadn't had a chance to talk to her since before the calf-roping event. She had just disappeared from the bleachers, and he lost her in the crowd. By the time he spotted her again, she was busy carrying food out from the kitchen to the picnic area.

Even from a distance, he could see her fatigue. Damn, she'd probably been working since dawn. Well, he was about to do something about that.

He marched over to her, and before she had a chance to escape to the kitchen again, took her aside. "I thought we were going to spend the day together," he said.

With a long sigh, Josie brushed delicate strands of raven hair from her face. "I can't now. I promised to help set out the food."

"How about I get you some help?" he suggested. "Then we can eat together."

"Travis, if you look around there are a lot of hungry people waiting."

"And you've been doing more than your share of work," he said. "You need to sit down and not overdo it." He searched her face. She looked so tired. "Let me help."

She finally nodded, and he followed her into the kitchen. Several women filled the spacious room, organizing the dozens of potluck dishes. How hard could it be to transfer the food outside?

"You go into the other room and rest," he told her. "I can handle this."

She started to argue. "But…"

"You want me to carry you in there?"

She shook her head, then started out of the room. He took a moment to enjoy the view of her cute backside in jeans, before he turned away and rolled up his sleeves. "Okay, ladies what do I need to do?"

Mrs. Foster, his tenth-grade teacher, smiled at him. "Why, Travis Randell, are you wanting to help?"

"Yes, ma'am, that's what I planned."

The gray-haired woman placed her hands on her ample hips. "Still trying to impress the girls, I see."

He grinned. "How am I doin'?"

For an answer the older woman shoved a big bowl of salad at him, then another filled with something made with gelatin. "Take these outside and give them to Thelma Brown. We'll make sure that Josie takes a break."

"Thanks." Travis headed out the door, and soon returned for more. Thirty minutes later, he'd made several trips. Once everyone seemed to be content, he walked to the grill and requested a steak, medium rare, and a piece of barbecued chicken. Then he loaded two plates with salads and rolls. After retrieving a couple of sodas, he walked to the house, but avoided the kitchen, detouring through the French doors in the living room. That's where he found Josie. She was sound asleep on the sofa.

He managed to place his bounty on the coffee table, then pulled the sodas from under his arm. He silenced a groan caused by the bruises he'd incurred from today's events, Travis sat down on the floor. He was a little disappointed he'd be dining alone. But he knew Josie was exhausted and needed to rest. Ella had told him how hard she'd been working since dawn to help get things ready.

He cut into his steak and took a bite. His appetite faded as he looked at Josie's pretty face. She seemed so peaceful, he wanted to curl up beside her and just hold her.

Lord, he was losing it.

A few months ago, he would have been bored to death sitting around, or competing in a neighborhood rodeo for a silly ribbon. Now, all he wanted was to spend some time with Josie. Just holding her, stroking her, loving her. His body began to stir. Watch it, he warned himself, remembering how quickly things had gotten out of hand the other night.

As if she were reading his thoughts, Josie's eyes opened, and she sat up. "Oh, what happened?"

"I think you decided you needed a nap. Sorry, did I wake you?"

She shook her head and rubbed her eyes. "Why are you here?"

He was surprised that she didn't know how much he wanted to be with her. "Because you are."

"But you should be outside with your family. I don't want to keep you from them."

With his battered body protesting, Travis moved up to the edge of the sofa. "Josie, this is where I want to be. With you." He raised an eyebrow. "Unless you don't want me here."

Josie knew a lie would be best for everyone. She should make him go away. Not let him know how much she wanted him with her. How much she wanted to depend on him. Instead, she told Travis what was in her heart. "No, please stay."

"Good." He leaned close and placed a soft kiss on her lips. "Now, you need to eat. I brought you some grilled chicken, but I have plenty of steak. We can share if you like." He cut a piece, stabbed it with his fork, then brought it to her mouth.

Josie opened and bit into the flavorful meat. She moaned her satisfaction. "This is wonderful."

"Circle B beef. Prime choice. Hank has a steer butchered every year for the rodeo." He cut another portion and fed it to her.

"Stop, I'm eating all your steak."

"So, you need the iron. Besides, I like feeding you," he said. "I bet you haven't eaten today." Without waiting for her reply, he handed her a plate. "Better start catching up, or your baby is going to complain."

The thought made Josie laugh, then suddenly her gaze locked with Travis's brown eyes. Her breathing caught. There was hunger in his look and it had nothing to do with food. The man wanted her, and Josie knew that if she wasn't careful, she was going to get hurt. Travis was tempting her with something she hadn't had much of in her life. Male attention.

She averted her gaze. "I'm glad things turned out well in Houston," she began.

He scooped up a forkful of potato salad. "Are you curious to know the details?"

Josie felt heat rush to her face. "It's none of my business. I only meant—"

"It's okay, Josie," he said. "I have nothing to hide from you. On the advice from my lawyer, Matt Hayes, I went to Houston. Lisa and Byron had been found and the D.A. needed my statement to prosecute. I'll have to return again for the trial, but as far as I'm concerned, I don't want any more to do with Houston."

"What about your business?"

"Private Access doesn't exist anymore. Thanks to Lisa and Byron it's gone." He shrugged. "I salvaged as much as possible, then came home."

"I'm sorry, Travis." She could see the sadness in his eyes and wanted to reach out and comfort him. "I know you worked hard to build your company."

He nodded. "I did. But the hardest part was facing the people who betrayed me. Two people I'd trusted. They used me. Would you believe that Lisa had the nerve to use the fact that I loved her?" His gaze met Josie's. "She tried to use that to barter with, to make me forget what she did."

"Do you still love her?" Josie found herself asking.

He shook his head. "How could I, after all the lies, the broken trust?"

Josie tensed, seeing Travis's anger. How would he feel about her secret? Would he think she betrayed him, too? She never wanted to find out. For that reason alone, she couldn't stay much longer.

Travis was surprised by Josie's question, but happy she cared enough to ask. To be honest, he hadn't invested much time into his relationship with Lisa. Not as much as he should have, but still the pain was there. He'd been used, and he didn't know if he could ever trust again. But then there was Josie. He'd thought about her all the time he was in Houston. Life had kicked her a few times, but her tenacity and stubbornness kept her going. He respected that, but mostly he respected her honesty. He told himself that he couldn't risk his heart again, but looking at Josie made him forget all his doubts.

He shook his head. "I don't think I ever loved Lisa. When she walked into my life, I think we were both feeling needy and didn't want to be alone."

Josie nodded. "So what are your plans now?"

Travis had been thinking about that one a long time. "I truly don't know. I have my security patents and Matt says there's a company interested in leasing them. If that happens, money won't be a problem, but it also doesn't leave me much to do."

"What about the guest ranch? I thought Chance and Cade wanted you to run the operation?"

Ah, that was the sixty-four-thousand-dollar question. Years ago, he'd left San Angelo wanting to make something of himself. To leave behind the stigma of his father's mistakes. But both Chance and Cade had settled down and made a good life here. Travis found he wanted the same thing. He looked at Josie and his body heated up instantly. He wanted it very much.

"I'm not sure I'm cut out for the job," he said, honestly. "I'm a computer nerd. Byron was the one who handled promoting our services. I just kept the computers up and running.''

''You don't give yourself enough credit.'' Her eyes met his. ''I watched you charm the crowd today. I think you can do anything you set your mind to.''

His pulse sped up. ''So you think I'm charming?''

She bit her lip. ''I think you're fishing for a compliment.''

''Nope, just fishing for a kiss.'' He leaned closer, trying to control his hunger. ''Think you can give me one?''

That was Josie's problem. She ached to give Travis what he was asking for. ''I'm sure there are dozens of women who would be willing to accommodate you. Why me?''

Travis couldn't believe that she had no idea how beautiful she was, inside and out. He reached for her; his hand cupped the back of her neck and tilted her face to his. ''Let me see…perhaps it's your incredible eyes, that seem to change color with your mood. Right now they're a sexy green. Or maybe it's your cute nose.'' His gaze moved lower. ''No, it's definitely your mouth,'' he said huskily as his finger slid along her lower lip. ''It's just too inviting. Makes me hungry just to look at you.''

Josie was unable to breathe and was getting lightheaded. ''Oh, Travis. You shouldn't say that.''

''Why? It's true. I want you, all of you, Josie.'' His head dipped and he captured her mouth. He wanted nothing more than to devour her, but instead he fought to keep the kiss light, so as not to frighten her. He could wait. He could be patient awhile longer, until Josie could trust him. But hearing her soft whimper was his undoing. He deepened the kiss, pushing his tongue inside to taste and stroke her.

A band started to play outside, but all Travis was tuned in to was Josie. Finally he broke off the kiss as a twangy ballad filled the room. Silently, he removed the plate from Josie's lap, then he stood and drew her into his arms.

"What are you doing?"

He looked hurt. "If you can't recognize my fancy footwork, Ella is going to be so sad when she finds out her dance lessons were a waste."

She looked down at his black Roper boots. "Ella taught you to dance?"

"She taught all of us."

Travis drew Josie into his arms and held her close. He shuddered when her soft curves molded against his body, as if she were sculpted for him. He closed his eyes and reveled in the feeling of her nearness. He wanted Josie more than just physically. He wanted all of her—body and soul.

Without breaking his hold, he whispered in her ear. "Josie, I know you've been hurt in the past, but I promise to stay by your side. I want to be a part of your life and your baby's."

She looked up at him. "Travis—"

He placed a finger over her lips. "I know, it's too soon. But just so you know, I'm going to be there for you. So just take your time to think about us. I told you earlier that I wouldn't press you."

He placed a kiss against her lips. It didn't take long before things intensified. The dance forgotten, his arms tightened around her, pulling her against him. Then unable to take the torture any longer, he released her.

He pressed his forehead against Josie's. "Maybe it would be a good idea to go outside and be with the family," he suggested.

"You should spend time with Hank."

"Not without you. Josie, how can I make you understand that I want to be with you?"

Her gaze darted away. "It's not a good idea, Travis. People will think—"

"What will people think? That I care about you? I do care, Josie, a lot."

"But I'm pregnant, and people will know soon enough," she said. "They might think that you're…"

A strange feeling settled in his gut at the thought of fathering her child. He found he liked the idea. "That I'm the father? Would that be so bad? Unless it bothers you that my own life has been splashed across all the Houston papers?" He stepped back. "I'm sorry Josie, I didn't think…" For years he'd run from the shame his daddy had brought the Randell name. Twenty years later, he'd done it, too.

"Oh, no, Travis, it's not that," she said, placing her hand on his arm, stopping him from leaving her. "I'm trying to protect you. You don't need me or my baggage."

There was a strange stirring in his chest as the realization hit him. He wanted it all, Josie and the baby. Whatever she was willing to give him he would take. He drew her close again. "Don't say that, Josie. God, I'd feel proud if people thought I was your little one's father." His hand moved to cover her stomach as he realized how much he meant the words.

Josie closed her eyes against the onslaught of emotions that threatened her resolve. "Oh, Travis, you can't mean that." She didn't want to love this man.

"Why? It's true."

"Because I can't handle it. Not now."

"I don't want you to handle anything, Josie. I just want you to be happy, and to trust me not to hurt you."

"I want to believe you, but life has proved me wrong too many times."

He smiled. "Give me time, sweet lady, I'm going to change your mind." His head dipped toward her and he captured her mouth in a kiss that held the promise of all her dreams.

Oh, how Josie wanted to believe him.

The next morning Travis and his brothers awoke early to help clean up after the rodeo. That was all right with Travis; he needed to stay busy. Josie had him so confused he couldn't sleep. He understood how she might be gun-shy about a relationship, but he knew she cared about him.

He and Chance had finished storing the tables in the shed and watched the rental company truck pull away with the extra tables and chairs. Things were getting back to normal again.

"Well, looks like we're about finished," Chance said. "I should head home. Joy and I were up most of the night with Katie. She's cutting a tooth."

"You got a minute?" Travis asked.

"Sure. What's on your mind?" Chance tipped his hat back, and his sandy hair fell across his forehead. The once serious oldest brother now looked happy and easygoing. Travis credited his better mood to Joy.

"I got a problem."

Chance frowned. "I thought you said your lawyer was handling everything."

"He is. That's not the problem." He looked around the deserted area. The nearest people were two hands busy working in the corral. "It's Josie," Travis blurted out.

A smile creased Chance's face. "So, you're finally admitting you have feelings for the woman."

Travis blew out a long breath. "Has everyone around here been watching us?"

"Well the family has noticed how much attention you pay to her. You spent the evening with her last night, danced every dance. You wouldn't let another man near her."

"Would you let anyone near Joy?"

"Hell, no." Chance laughed. "You're as bad as Cade and I were. We both pretty much made fools of ourselves before we admitted our feelings." His expression grew serious. "But let me give you some advice. If you care about Josie don't waste any time. We Randells seem to fall hard and fast."

"I've already made one mistake," Travis said. "How do I know if I'm about to make another?"

"You don't." His brother sighed and pushed back his hat. "Now, I've never met this Lisa you were engaged to, but from what you told me, I have a feeling she's nothing like us. I think you would have discovered that sooner or later."

Travis thought back to a year ago and the aggressive woman who had walked into his office. Not only had she gotten a job, but within weeks she was in his bed. Lisa had manipulated the situation to get everything she wanted. He was just a stepping stone.

"No, she never wanted a family," Travis said, unable to believe he went along with it. "Kids weren't even up for discussion."

"She must have been a hell of a looker to get you to change your way of thinking so drastically."

Travis nodded. "She was good," he admitted. "So good, she was able to play me off against Byron." He let out a long breath. "Boy, I'm lucky I got out of that mess."

"You were lucky, but it's still keeping you from moving on with your life...with Josie. If it's of any help, both Joy and Abby think she's pretty special and perfect for you."

"Jeez, it's nice to have everyone's approval."

Chance smiled. "Sorry, that's what happens when you're part of a family. We love you, and want you to be happy."

Travis felt his throat tighten. "There was a time I didn't think I needed that." He looked his brother in the eyes. "I've learned a lot the past few months, and without the family, I don't think I could have gotten through this."

Chance smacked him on the back. "If you don't know by now, I'm here to tell you, we're proud of you, Travis. And we'll be lucky if you decide to manage the Mustang Valley Guest Ranch."

Travis had been thinking about it, too. He wanted to come home. But he had reservations. "You're not just making up this job so I'll stay?"

Chance grinned. "You always were suspicious. Wait a few weeks after we've put you to work. You're family so we can abuse you. And since I'm the oldest, I get to boss you around."

Travis grinned at his brother's teasing. "Like hell. I believe in your family Joy is the boss now."

"And I wouldn't have it any other way," the oldest Randell stated.

There was no doubt both his brothers were happy and settled, and Travis wanted the same. "I think I'd like to try it," he said.

"That's great." Chance grabbed him in a tight embrace. A few years ago, the show of affection would have bothered Travis; now he reveled in it.

Chance pulled away. "Now go and convince Josie that you can't live without her." Then this brother paused as his brows drew together. "Your hesitation doesn't have anything to do with the baby, does it?"

Travis shook his head. He was actually excited. "As far as I'm concerned the baby is a bonus. I think we've all learned the hard way that blood doesn't make you good parents."

His brother agreed.

"It's Josie who's shying away. I'm not sure she'll ever let herself depend on another man."

"Then you better get busy and convince her you're not going to walk out on her because the brochure is nearly finished. That means so is her job."

"I know," Travis said as he walked his brother to the truck. "Somehow, I'm going to find a way to keep her here until she admits we have a future together." He only wished he felt as confident as he sounded.

After a day off, Josie arrived at the ranch house the next afternoon to really work. She'd been a little surprised that she hadn't heard from or seen Travis yesterday. But after the rodeo, he'd told her she needed sleep and ordered her not to do anything but relax. Josie hadn't slept late in years. All her life she had worked, and the diner had been open every day of the week, so Josie was there. Then when her mother got sick, Josie ran things by herself. She wasn't used to taking it easy, but she quickly discovered a few extra hours of sleep was heavenly—that was, after she got Travis Randell out of her thoughts.

Josie entered the empty kitchen and called out. No one answered. She walked through the familiar house to the den where she was to meet Travis. Her heart rate sped up in anticipation of seeing him. She couldn't deny she missed him and was more than a little disappointed he hadn't stopped by the cabin. Maybe if she'd invited him, he would have come.

No, she didn't need to encourage him. As she reached the den music drifted through the doors. Someone was singing a country song.

She stopped in the doorway to watch Travis leaning over the computer, belting out the words as if he had sung it many times before. She enjoyed the richness of his voice but not as much as the sight of the man himself. When he stood and reached for a folder, his T-shirt pulled taut over his broad shoulders and back. Her body tingled with awareness, even more so as her gaze moved down to his narrow waist and tight rear end. The way he filled out his jeans was sinful. This was no computer nerd.

As if he sensed her presence, Travis turned around. Still singing along to the song, he walked across the room, drew her into his arms and started dancing. Josie laughed, making it difficult to keep up with the fast two-step.

When the song ended, he relinquished his hold. "Did you rest yesterday?"

She nodded. "And I slept an extra two hours this morning."

"Good. I got up at five. I was thinking about you, all cozy and warm under the blankets." He leaned closer and tugged on her long braid. "And wishing I was there with you. But I figured you wouldn't be getting any sleep if that were the case."

She backed away. She didn't need to hear this. "Maybe you should tell me what you want to work on today."

"Trust."

She stared at him. "What?"

"I want you to trust me, Josie. I don't want you to be afraid of me."

"I'm not afraid of you," she denied.

"But you are. You're afraid I'm going to hurt you."

She had to glance away. "We've discussed this before. I'm only here for a little while longer."

"What if I want you to stay?" he asked. "What if I want you and the baby to make the Circle B your home?"

She shook her head. No! She couldn't stay, not on the ranch with Hank.... "I can't," she said. "Maybe in town."

He folded his arms. "What if I can make it so you can stay here?"

"Travis, the brochure is nearly done. The fact is, you don't need me now." He'd been asking for more and more pictures, pictures he didn't really need.

"Your photos are going to be used. Abby is talking about a calendar. But I had another job in mind."

"What job?"

He stepped back and sat on the edge of the desk, then folded his arms across his chest. "As the new manager of the guest ranch I can hire whoever I need."

She gasped. "Oh, Travis, you decided to take the job!"

He smiled as he nodded. "Like I was saying, as the new manager, I'm going to need someone to run the office."

Hope surged through her. Could she possibly do this? "But...I've never run an office. And I've had no computer training."

"We have plenty of time before the spring opening to train you. And there are good health benefits, too. So you don't have to worry about how you're going to pay for the hospital when the baby comes."

Josie felt the tears well in her eyes. Why did Travis have to be so nice to her? It made leaving more difficult, and darn it, she had to leave. "You can't create a job for me, Travis. I won't take charity. I've taken care of myself all my life, and I certainly will now."

Travis watched as Josie's chin came up, and she folded her arms in front of her. She was as stubborn as they came. So what if he did come up with this job? He was going to need help eventually anyway. But he couldn't lose her. Somehow he had to convince her to stay. He wanted to admit his feelings, but he was afraid she wouldn't believe him and truly take off. No, he had to try a different strategy.

"Well, I'm going to put an ad in the paper on Monday. If you don't take the job, someone else will. Better let go of your pride, Josie. Think about your baby."

"I *do* think about my baby." She blinked at the tears in her eyes. "That's all I think about. You don't know what it's like to have a life inside you and know that you have to feed and protect her."

"No, but I'm trying to help," he said. "It's not

charity. Truly it isn't. You'll be answering phones, taking reservations, hiring housekeepers and overseeing the cottages. And not just here, for Abby and Cade, but for Chance and Joy when the camping area opens on their property. It'll be too much work for one person. I need someone who can handle people, and I thought that with your experience at the diner you'd be perfect. But if you don't want the job…''

"I want it," she nearly shouted, then glanced away. "I'm sorry. I thought that you were—"

"Trying to get you to stay." He grinned. "You're right, I am. I'm not going to lie, Josie. In case you haven't noticed, I'm crazy about you."

He watched her eyes darken and knew she had feelings for him, too. Somehow he had to convince her that they would be great together. He stepped closer and lowered his head. "I'm going to wear you down, Josie." Just then another country song filled the room. And Travis drew her into his arms.

"Don't argue anymore, Josie, just feel what's between us. I'm going to persuade you that we belong together. Trust me." His mouth closed over hers, shutting off any more protest. At least for now.

Chapter Ten

The past two days had been hell. Travis gripped the steering wheel tighter as he drove down the highway toward Mustang Valley. He wasn't about to wait any longer to talk to Josie. She said she was staying, but for how long? She probably would find some excuse to leave, and if so, he was prepared to argue the point. There was no way he was going to let her go back to El Paso. Alone and pregnant. There was no one who cared about her. Not like he did.

Travis didn't know how or when it happened, and as much as he had tried not to let Josie matter to him, she did. A lot. Now, he couldn't let her walk out of his life.

He turned off onto the new road to the valley. The drive took him between rows of tall trees with bright sunlight filtering through the branches. He couldn't help but think about the first day he'd seen Josie. Although he'd fought it, he'd been attracted to her even then, but pure stubbornness kept him from seeing she was the best thing that had happened to him. He knew now, and he couldn't let her go. He pulled to a stop at the gravel parking area about two hundred yards back from the valley and a hundred yards from the cabins. He would have to make the rest of the journey on foot. That was probably a good thing because he needed time to think about what to say to Josie.

How to convince her to stay and marry him.

Josie had been pacing the cabin ever since Travis's phone call, twenty minutes ago. She didn't know if her constant movement helped at all, but it was better than sitting and worrying about what to do. She'd had two days and still hadn't been able to decide. Two choices were open to her: she could leave and never tell Hank who she really was, or stay and take a chance with the truth.

If she did stay, she could lose Travis. He would never forgive her for withholding her true identity. She thought back to the day in the office when he'd admitted he was crazy about her. She'd wanted to admit her feelings, too. That she loved him to distraction. She'd never dreamed she could feel this way about anyone.

Suddenly dread washed over her. And what about Hank? How would he feel about a woman claiming to be his daughter showing up at this time in his life? Would he think she was just after something?

Oh, God. She sank down into the kitchen chair. The last thing she wanted was for Hank to resent her. They'd developed a good relationship over the past few weeks. Tears pooled in her eyes. That was more than Josie had ever hoped for. And that was enough

for her. A father had never been part of her life, so
how could she miss what she didn't have? She drew
another breath and touched her stomach. The one who
would lose was her child. Josie wanted to give her
child grandparents. That wasn't going to happen, so
she had to stop torturing herself.

The sound of knocking broke into her thoughts.
She drew a strengthening breath and went to answer
the door. She'd been expecting Travis and wasn't surprised to see him standing on the porch. But the sight
of the man still caused her throat to suddenly go dry.
His broad shoulders were covered by a starched white
shirt tucked into a pair of nicely fitted ink-black jeans.
In his hands, he held his black Stetson. Her gaze
raised to the sun-streaked hair that fell across his forehead making a contrast with his dark-chocolate eyes.
She ached to reach out and stroke the small cleft in
his chin, but resisted. She couldn't allow herself to
touch him, or her resolve would vanish.

"Travis." She stepped aside to let him inside.

He accepted her invitation and walked into the
cabin. In one swift movement, he tossed his hat on
the table, then reached for her, pulling her tight
against him. A soft gasp broke from her as she allowed him to take her hands and put them around his
neck, just as his head bent toward hers.

Then his hungry mouth claimed hers, taking long,
deep kisses, and she clung to him. Her body burned
as he stroked her from her waist to her breasts. When
his hands covered her nipples they quickly beaded
against his palms. She whimpered at the sheer ec-
stasy.

He tore his mouth from hers. "I've missed you,
Josie." He rained kisses over her face. "These past

two days have been hell. Please, tell me that you've been miserable, too.''

She wanted nothing more than to confess her feelings to him. ''I've missed you, too.'' She stood on her toes and pressed her mouth to his. This time she revealed her hunger as her tongue teased him, sliding along his lower lip. He opened readily as she slipped inside timidly, drawing a deep groan from Travis. He tightened his hold and returned the favor. This time she was the one who moaned.

He pulled back, his eyes dark with desire. ''We can't keep going on like this, Josie,'' he said breathlessly. ''I want you too much just to be satisfied with stolen moments. I want a life with you. I want to marry you.''

Whatever Travis had expected from Josie, it wasn't reluctance. But she suddenly stiffened in his arms. Damn. He'd known she was unprepared for his marriage proposal, but he thought she cared about him.

''Travis, you don't know what you're asking. We barely know each other.''

''Josie, time has nothing to do with it. I care about you. And I thought you cared for me.''

''I do. But…marriage?''

Although Travis resisted letting her go, she slipped from his arms. ''Josie, if you're worried…I mean, I would love the baby as if it were mine.''

''Oh, Travis…'' she cried as tears flooded her eyes.

''Hey, I didn't mean to make you cry,'' he said, feeling panicked. ''I guess I read you wrong. I thought you felt the way I did.'' He started to turn away when she reached for him.

''I *do* care about you, Travis. It would be a lot

easier if I didn't. But this is such a big step. Please...I need some time to think about it."

Travis didn't like the idea of waiting, but agreed. "Just promise me you won't take off."

"Promise. I need to think some things through. Alone."

"Can't I hang around and try to convince you?" he teased.

Josie shook her head and gave him a half smile. "We both need time."

His hand covered hers. "No, Josie, I don't need any time. I know exactly what I want. You."

Josie wanted to scream that she wanted him, too. But the words stuck in her throat. She couldn't say anything until the truth was out. "I promise I won't take long."

He kissed her nose. "I'm going to Chance's. We're having a meeting with Cade. I'll have my cell phone with me just in case you need me."

I need you every minute of every day, she cried silently. "Okay, I promise I'll call you," she said, nudging him toward the door. If she didn't get rid of him soon, she was going to break down.

But Travis didn't go easily. At the door, he pulled her to him and kissed her hard and deep, assuring her again of his feelings. Josie feasted on him, too, knowing that it might be her last chance.

She finally broke off the kiss. "Goodbye, Travis."

He hesitated for a moment, staring at her with those mesmerizing coffee eyes. She trembled as she fought to resist him. It was hard, so hard that every cell in her body ached to return to the shelter of his arms and shut out the world. Somehow, she managed to pick up his hat from the table and hand it to him.

Travis took it and walked off. Then the door closed, and Josie sank against it. She drew several breaths as she fought back tears. With the sound of the truck driving off, she went into the alcove. Opening the dresser drawer, she pulled out her mother's letter. It was time she talked to Hank. No matter what, it was time he knew he had a daughter.

Josie arrived at the Circle B thirty minutes later. She parked by the back door and climbed out of her car. Taking the opportunity, she glanced around at the state-of-the-art ranch Hank had spent years building. It would have been wonderful to grow up here, she thought as a lonely ache settled in her chest. But this wasn't her home, no matter how badly she wanted to belong.

She walked up the steps and through the back door into the kitchen where she found Ella folding laundry.

She smiled. "Well, hello, Josie. I didn't know you were coming by this morning."

"I didn't mean to disturb you, Ella. I—I just needed to see Hank for a few minutes."

"Child, you don't ever disturb me. I wish you were around more often." The housekeeper frowned. "Are you getting lonely out there in the cabin?"

Josie tried to hide her nervousness. "No, I'm fine. It's beautiful out there. A photographer's dream. I was able to get really close to one of the mustangs yesterday. I'll let you see the pictures when they're developed." But Josie wondered if she'd be around then.

"I'd like that," the housekeeper said.

"Well, I think I'll go see Hank. Is he in the study?" At Ella's nod Josie walked through the sunny yellow kitchen and the formal dining room with its oak trestle table and high-back chairs. Emotion tugged at her heart as she remembered the meals she'd shared in here with Hank and the family. Struggling to keep her focus, she continued into the huge room where Hank liked to watch the big-screen television and play with the grandkids. Her chest tightened more as she wondered if her baby would ever be considered one of them.

Her steps slowed at the sight of the open study door. Her mind screamed for her to leave, but her heart made her continue on. This could be her one chance to put things right. She drew another breath and peered through the doorway where she found Hank at the desk, his head bent as he read something. She gazed lovingly at the man, from his thick gray hair to his tan, sun-weathered face. He was still handsome at sixty-five, with kind hazel eyes and a smile that put everyone at ease.

He glanced up, then stood. "Josie, how long have you been here?"

"I just got here." She tried to slow her breathing. "There's something I need to talk to you about."

"Sure," he said, and came around the desk. He took her hand and guided her to two rust-colored chairs. She sat down and he joined her. "What do you need?"

Josie closed her eyes for a second. "I don't need anything. You've been very generous to me these past weeks. There's something I need to tell you, though...."

Hank frowned. "If it's about leaving, I want you to know that you can stay here as long as you need."

She wanted to weep over his kindness. "That's

very kind of you. But I'm not sure you'll feel that way when you discover that I haven't been totally honest with you. I mean, from the beginning I should have told you who I was.''

"You're not Josie Gutierrez?''

"Yes, that's my name, but...'' she began. With Hank's confused look, she reached into her purse, took out the letter and handed it to him. "You sent this to my mother.''

Josie got up and walked across the room. She stared out though the windowed doors, wanting to give Hank time to absorb the news. It didn't take long.

"You're Elissa Romero's daughter?'' His voice was hoarse with emotion.

Josie turned to see a soft smile, but she knew it would disappear after she delivered the rest of the news. "Yes, I'm her daughter. But...I'm also your daughter. My mother got pregnant one of those weekends you spent with her.''

Hank's smile faded and a multitude of expressions flashed over his face. Then silently he stood and walked to her. She trembled as his gaze moved over her face. "You look like Elissa. So beautiful.'' He reached out and touched her cheek. "My daughter. I can't believe this. All these years. Why? Why didn't she ever let me know?''

Josie glanced down at the paper in his hand. "The letter. You told her that you didn't want to see her again.''

He, glanced at the yellowed paper, then back at her. "But you're my daughter. Oh, my God, you're my daughter.''

"It's a lie!'' an angry voice rang out.

They both turned to find a furious-looking Travis standing in the doorway. The last thing Josie wanted was for him to find out this way, but it was too late. "Travis, I thought you were at Chance's," she said.

He glared at her. "That would have made this more convenient for you, wouldn't it? Too bad I forgot some papers for the meeting." He folded his arms over his chest. "I guess I interrupted your plans."

"I was going to tell you, but I thought Hank deserved to know first."

"The hell you were!"

Hank stepped in. "Travis, stop it. This doesn't concern you," he said.

"It concerns me if someone's trying to use you. Someone's been lying to us from the start. Believe me, I know what that's like."

"No, Travis, you don't understand," Josie pleaded. "I had to tell the truth—to tell Hank who I was. I never wanted to hurt anyone, but when you asked me to marry you, I had to tell the truth. But Hank deserved to hear it first."

"Yeah, I bet you got a good laugh from that one," Travis snapped. His jaw clenched, his gaze cold and hard. "You're going for higher stakes. Well, I'm not letting you come here and lay claim to this ranch. So you can just pack your bags and leave."

"That's enough!" Hank shouted as he stepped in and faced Travis. "I told you this is between Josie and me."

"No, it's not." Josie drew a shaky breath. This was what she wanted to avoid. "I never wanted this to happen," she cried, fighting her tears. "I'll leave," she announced and started for the door. Even with Hank trying to stop her, she couldn't stay. Not with the angry look on Travis's face. She'd known the risk she was taking by telling Hank, but she'd never thought that Travis would react so hatefully.

Somehow Josie managed to make it to her car before the tears came, but she knew it would be a long time before they stopped.

Hank turned on Travis. "I hope you're proud of yourself," he said once they were alone.

"Come on, Hank. You don't even know for sure that Josie was telling the truth."

Hank stared at him. "She *is* telling the truth. I *did* spend weekends with Elissa Romero."

A surprised Travis hesitated. "Well, that doesn't mean she's your daughter."

Hank had no doubt Josie was his. In his heart, he knew. "If Elissa told Josie I'm her father, then I am. God, Travis, have you ever looked into Josie's eyes? She has my eyes." He cursed under his breath, then started out of the room. He had to find her.

"Where are you going?" Travis asked.

"To find my daughter," he called over his shoulder, loving the sound of the word. *Daughter.* He had a daughter. He rushed out of the house and didn't stop until he was in his truck. He started up the vehicle and headed for the valley. He had to reach Josie to tell her how much he wanted her here.

Ten minutes later, he reached the cabin and let out a breath when he saw the light on. On the porch, he knocked and waited anxiously until she finally opened the door.

When he saw Josie's red eyes, he cursed Travis again. "Please, can we talk?"

"Maybe we shouldn't," she said. "I'll just go back to El Paso."

"And live where?" he asked. "You have no family."

"I have a few friends who can help me out for a while. Oh, Hank, I never wanted…" Their eyes met, and she swallowed hard. Her voice broke as she spoke, "I didn't come here to cause you any trouble."

Hank stepped over the threshold and took her into his arms. "Oh, my dear girl, you could never do that." He held her tight.

"I just wanted to see you…once. See what you were like," she confessed in a teary whisper. "When I rode to the valley that first time, I meant to keep it at that. I was planning to leave when I hurt my ankle."

Hank pulled back, trying to see her through his own tears. "Then I'm glad now you had to stay. I would hate to think I might have missed knowing you."

"Really?" she asked brushing away her tears.

He nodded. "I knew you were special the first time I laid eyes on you. I just wish you told me sooner." He gripped her shoulders. "But I understand," he told her, then suddenly he began to grin. "I can't believe this. You're my daughter. You'll never know how much I wanted a child."

"Then why didn't you come back to my mother?" she asked timidly. "Surely you knew there was a chance that you made her pregnant?"

Hank shook his head, then he released Josie and sank down in the chair at the table. "Mae and I never had children. I just took for granted it was my problem. When my wife died, I was so lonely. When I met Elissa…" He ran his fingers through his hair in frustration. "God, you must hate me. Your mother having to raise you by herself. If I had only known, Josie. I swear I would have been there for you. For Elissa."

Josie sat down opposite him. "I know that now."

He reached out and touched her face, unable to believe the miracle. "What a wonderful surprise you are. And so beautiful."

Josie glanced away shyly. "Oh, yes. It's every man's dream to have his daughter appear on his doorstep and pregnant to boot."

"Hey, you're talking about my grandchild." Hank didn't think his heart could get any fuller, but it did. "Finding out I'm a father and grandfather in the same day, oh, my, this just gets better and better."

"You're happy?"

He kissed her forehead. "Oh, Josie, that doesn't begin to express how I feel at this moment." He couldn't keep the tears from his eyes. "You're my daughter." He said the words as if he had trouble believing them. "I hope you don't mind if I tell you I already love you."

All her life, Josie had longed to hear those words from the man she ached to call father. "When I was a little girl, I dreamed about meeting my dad. I even pretended that he was looking for me." She couldn't contain her tears as they spilled over and ran down her cheek. "And one day he was going to come for me and my mother." She swallowed as she searched Hank's face, seeing his sadness. "And now I found you. Oh, Hank, I feel the same way about you," she managed to say.

Hank pulled her into a tight embrace, and Josie hung on tight. How much time passed she didn't know or care. Finally Hank pulled back and looked at her. "I'm so sorry I wasn't there for you when you were growing up." He sucked in a long breath. "But I'm here now. And I'm going to take care of you. First, you're going to move back to the house."

"I can't," she moaned. Her chest constricted from the pain that she couldn't go with him. "I won't interrupt your life, Hank. You have family to consider." Never again did she want to see Travis's hatred. She had no choice but to leave. "I can't stay."

"But I just found you," Hank said. "How can I let you go? Chance, Cade and Travis will come love you. I know Travis does already. He's just in shock. He'll get over his anger."

She shook her head. "I understand why he despises me. I lied to him. I just hope one day, he'll forgive me. Please, Hank, don't make this any harder on me. The last thing I want to do is make you choose sides. No, I won't split up your family."

"But you're my family, too. I want to get to know you." He hugged her. "Please, Josie, this can work out."

She wanted to believe him so badly, but she wasn't holding out false hope. "I think it would be best if I move into town."

"No, not yet. Give it a few days. At least let me talk to the boys."

She heard the urgency in Hank's voice and couldn't deny him. "Okay, but don't get your hopes up. I don't see Travis coming around."

Hank smiled. "Just let me handle Travis. He may be stubborn, but he isn't foolish enough to let you go."

* * *

Right after Hank had taken off after Josie, he'd made a call to Chance's and asked him and Cade to come to the house. They had a right to know what was going on. Travis was pacing the study when a truck pulled up out front, then another.

It wasn't long before he heard the sound of boots against the hardwood floors as his brothers entered the house. Then Chance and Cade appeared in the study.

"Okay, what the hell is going on?" Chance asked. "You sounded like it was an emergency. It better be because I have to be at a horse auction in Midland tomorrow, early."

"It is," Travis said. "Hank needs our help."

A concerned-looking Cade crossed the room. "What the hell is it?"

Travis started to tell them when Hank walked in. His gaze went to Travis. "I think I should be the one to tell them," he said.

"Will *someone* tell us?" Chance asked impatiently.

They all turned to Hank and waited for him to start. The older man drew a long breath, then said, "Josie Gutierrez is my daughter."

Stunned silence blanketed the room as brother looked at brother, acting as if they hadn't heard right. Finally Chance spoke up, "Josie is your daughter? How? When?"

Hank cocked an eyebrow. "Since you three were brought up on a ranch, I don't think I need to go into the details." He slipped his hands into his jeans pockets. "It was several months after Mae's death, before you boys came to the ranch. I went on a cattle-buying trip to El Paso where I met Elissa Romero. Our...

relationship only lasted a few months." He glanced up at the three brothers. "I felt…I was betraying Mae. So I wrote Elissa a letter and told her I couldn't see her again."

Chance started the conversation. "So that's the reason you never knew about Josie."

Hank nodded.

Travis didn't see the anger from Cade and Chance that he'd expected. "Don't you think it's awfully convenient that Josie showed up here all of a sudden?" he asked.

"Why is that?" Cade asked Hank.

"Elissa never told Josie about me until right before she died a few months ago," Hank said. "She gave her a letter I sent breaking off the relationship."

Chance shook his head. "What a shame to lose all those years." He smiled. "But at least you're together now. Wow, a daughter."

"So that means you have no problem with Josie being here?" Hank asked. "I mean, it doesn't change anything with us."

Both Chance and Cade looked at each other and shrugged. "Hell, no, but I wish she'd been around all these years to share the chores," Cade offered. "Well, I guess we'll just work her harder now." With a teasing grin, he patted Hank on the back. "Congratulations, *Dad.*"

"Thanks, boys," Hank said. "I'm pretty happy about the situation myself."

Travis stood back not believing what was going on. Was he the only one who was concerned that Josie had lied? That she'd kept her identity a secret. She couldn't be trusted.

"Oh, wait until Joy and Abby find out there's going to be another woman around,'' Chance said. ''They'll love it.''

Hank's smile faded. ''I'm not sure I can get Josie to stay.''

''What do you mean?'' Cade asked. ''She's going to work at the guest ranch.''

Hank shook his head. ''She doesn't want to cause any trouble with the family.''

''What trouble can she cause?'' Chance asked.

''Well, hell, she's been lying to us from the beginning,'' Travis said.

Chance turned to Travis. ''If I remember correctly, that first day in the Valley you were interrogating her pretty heavily.''

''She still should have told us who she was,'' he insisted.

''Cut her some slack, bro,'' Chance said. ''From what I understand life hasn't been that easy on her. Has it been too long ago for us to remember what that's like? Surely we can be sympathetic.'' He stared at Travis, as if daring him to forget how it had been for them. How cruelly people had treated the Randell boys. He waved his arm. ''I've got to get home. We'll talk about this some more later.''

''Me, too,'' Cade announced and followed Chance. ''Tell Josie, welcome to the family.''

Travis wanted to leave, too, but he knew Hank needed to talk to him. ''Go ahead, and let me have it.''

Hank just looked at him. ''I'm not going to yell. You have your reasons for being upset with Josie, but I don't want you to use the excuse that you're trying to protect me. You're just trying to protect yourself.''

''I don't need any protection,'' Travis snapped.

"I've been through this before. Being used isn't new to me." Travis knew too well how capable Josie was of that.

"I think Josie has been the one who was hurt. I'm not exactly sure about her past, but I figure her stepfather hadn't behaved too loving toward her. And since she lost her mother, she's had no one else." He sighed. "What she must have thought about me for abandoning her."

Travis didn't need to hear this. He didn't want to think about the lonely little girl living in El Paso. About people being cruel to her.

"None of this is Josie's fault," Hank continued. "Her mother and I were to blame for the circumstances of her birth."

Travis wanted to stay angry at Josie. Damn! Why couldn't she have trusted him enough to tell him who she was? "Would you have married her mother if you'd known about the baby?"

Hank didn't hesitate to nod. "I loved Mae, and I truly cared about Elissa. I'd give anything to have a second chance to relive my decision to send that letter." He drew another long breath. "My only hope now is to have a chance to get to know my daughter." Hank's kind hazel eyes met Travis's. "Is that too much to ask?"

Travis knew Hank wasn't asking for much. He never did. From the first day the Randell brothers set foot on the Circle B, Hank Barrett had always been fair to them. All that he asked from Travis was the same fairness. He sighed. "No, it's not."

Chapter Eleven

He was acting like a jerk and he knew it.

Travis had been up most of the night with thoughts of Josie. He wanted to hate her for her deception, but the problem was he couldn't.

Before dawn he was up and in the barn, saddling Rocky. He needed a good hard ride to clear his head. Before he finished with the horse's tack, Chance walked into the barn.

"What the hell are you doing here?" Travis asked.

"I'm asking myself the same question. I left a warm bed and my beautiful wife to pound some sense into your thick head."

Great, big brother to the rescue. "Why don't you go back home and tell Joy you did your job?" he said as he swung the saddle over the gelding's back.

He shook his head. "I need to get to Midland so this is going to be quick. And so I expect some co-operation from you."

Not having a choice, Travis stopped his task and gave his brother his full attention. "Okay, have at it."

"You love Josie, so you might as well admit it."

"I'm not admitting anything."

Chance studied him a moment. "Damn, you're a Randell all right. Stubborn as they come. You might as well give in, Trav, because you can't live without her. Josie will be on your mind day and night. You can't sleep, that's why you're down here saddling Rocky, and you're going to ride this poor horse into the ground just to try to get the woman out of your head." Chance shook his head. "It isn't going to work. She's in your heart. We Randells are one-woman men."

Travis didn't want to hear this. "How do you know she's the one for me? I once loved Lisa."

"I doubt you ever looked at Lisa the way you look at Josie." Chance's expression told Travis that he knew what he was talking about. "Yeah, I saw how you followed her every move that first day. I almost laughed because it happened to me with Joy. I didn't even know Joy's name, and I was delivering her baby. But there was an instant connection. Then, there's Cade. He's loved Abby since high school. Even moving to Chicago couldn't get her out of his heart."

Travis knew everything his brother said was true. Josie had managed to get into his heart, a place he swore he wouldn't let anyone in. But she found the way. He cared about her more that he ever dreamed possible. He'd never felt this way. But if this was love, it sure hurt like hell. "But she didn't tell me who she was."

Chance shook his head. "I don't know about that. Maybe Josie was frightened. Frightened of being rejected again. I think that's something we all can understand. Hell, look what we went through. At least we had each other, and we were lucky enough to have Hank.'' Their eyes met. "Josie has no one. And she risked losing you to tell the truth. All she wants is to be loved, Travis. And she loves you enough to leave. Now, are you foolish enough to let the best thing that ever happened to you walk out of your life? To share her life with another man? Let another man be a father to her child?''

Travis didn't say anything. So many emotions flooded him. He couldn't imagine a life without Josie. Even after twenty years, he remembered what it was like to be alone. He didn't want that for her and the baby. Oh, God, what had he done?

His startled gaze shot to his brother. "Damn. What do I do? I said some pretty awful things.''

"Go to her. Get down on your knees if you have to. And just tell her what's in your heart. That's what's incredible about women, they're willing to forgive us even when we act stupid.''

Lord, he hoped so. "Thanks, bro,'' Travis said, then tightened the cinch on Rocky and led him out of the barn. He climbed on the horse and took off for Mustang Valley, praying Josie was willing to hear him out.

Travis stopped at the edge of the creek, not far from Josie's cabin. He dismounted and looked in the cabin window. She was gone but he was relieved to see her things were still there. He turned and led Rocky back to the stream. Crouching down, Travis cupped his hand and brought water to his mouth. After drinking his fill, he glanced around at the valley. The leaves had changed, leaving the valley in ribbons of bright fall colors. He'd bet Josie would have a heyday taking pictures here.

Damn. He had to find her. Raw emotions clawed at his throat as he remembered the first time he'd ever seen her. She was so beautiful. All that long raven hair and those large eyes. She battled him over and over, never backing down from him. He had desired her even then. Then over the last month he'd fallen the rest of the way. Now he was hopelessly in love with her.

Then out of stupid jealousy, he acted like a jackass and messed up everything. Had he ruined any chance that they could have a future together?

Suddenly he saw a movement from the corner of his eye that drew his attention. Travis stood up as he looked through the trees to the meadow where he saw a herd of mustangs...and Josie. His breath caught. She was dressed in faded jeans and a white blouse. Her raven hair hung free in waves down her back, nearly touching her waist. In her hand, she held her camera aimed at the ponies.

Josie hadn't been able to resist. She knew she shouldn't be out here with the mustangs, but all week they'd allowed her to get closer and closer. Each day, they trusted her more. She took shot after shot of the magnificent animals, knowing this could be her last chance. She'd come to love this valley and soon she'd have to leave.

Later today, Hank was driving her into town to find an apartment. He had talked her into staying around at least until the baby was born. She'd promised him that much. At least in San Angelo, she'd be around...the family. She still wasn't sure she could handle being so close to Travis. She closed her eyes, remembering how just days ago, he'd wanted to marry her. A sadness washed over her.

Now, he despised her.

No, she couldn't think about the negative. She had Hank…and her baby. Her hand covered her stomach protectively. That's all that mattered.

Josie took a step closer to the buckskin mare. When she didn't shy away, Josie reached out and touched her forehead. "Thatagirl." She gently stroked the mustang. "You want some attention, huh?" she crooned. "Don't we all."

The horse shook her head, then whinnied and jumped back. Josie turned to find the cause. Travis Randell stood at the edge of the meadow. He was in black jeans and a blue shirt and vest. His hat was tilted over his eyes, not giving her any clue to his mood. Josie knew from experience that it was best to stay away from him. She couldn't handle any more hurt.

"Josie, can I talk to you?" he called out.

"I think everything has been said, Travis." She started walking away from him, hoping to get back to the cabin without incident. Travis thought differently and followed her. Great. This was all she needed.

"Please, Travis. You don't need to order me off again. I'm leaving tomorrow. And I'm not taking a thing from Hank." She turned and marched off, but he didn't stop his pursuit.

"Josie, please," he called again. "Just hear me out."

She didn't stop. She couldn't handle another argument.

"I was wrong," he shouted.

That got her attention, and she swung around.

"I'm the one who should be leaving," he said. "You have more right to be here with Hank than I do."

"No, Travis. Hank loves you." Tears welled in her eyes. "You, Chance and Cade are his sons. I—I could never do that to him." As much as she fought to prevent it, she broke down. "I'm sorry, I never wanted to cause any trouble." She took off for the cabin, but before she could outrun him, he caught up to her. His grip was tight on her arm, and as much as she fought, she still ended up against his chest.

"Please, don't leave me," he begged. "I'm sorry, Josie. I was wrong about everything. I realize now why you didn't tell us who you were. You were afraid of exactly what happened. Just stay. The Circle B is your home. You belong here."

Not with him here. She couldn't bear it. "It won't work. You and me…"

"Oh, Josie, I want to make it better. Tell me what to do."

Love me, she screamed inside. "There's nothing to do. It wasn't meant to be," she said aloud.

His fists clenched in frustration. "Dammit, Josie, it was meant to be," he argued.

"That's not enough," she whispered, then ran off again and this time didn't stop until she reached the cabin. Once inside she let the tears fall as she sank down on her bed.

Travis burst through the door and heard Josie crying. Her sobs tore at his heart. He should leave her alone, but something drew him to her bedside. She was lying on her stomach, her face buried in the pillow. He sat down on the edge of the mattress.

"Josie," he whispered as he reached out and touched her back. She stiffened, but he didn't pull back. He couldn't.

"Go away," she pleaded.

"I can't. I tried but I can't leave you."

She sniffed and wiped her eyes. "Don't worry, Travis, I'll be fine. You don't have to take care of me anymore."

"It's not you I'm worried about, it's me. I don't think I can go on without you. I need you, Josie. Please, I know I acted like a jerk, and I said some awful things that I can never take back, but if you'll forgive me..."

He was shocked when she sat up, her eyes red and cheeks tearstained, but beautiful. "You'll what?" she asked.

He shrugged. "Whatever you want. I'll do whatever you want. Please just don't ask me to get out of your life. I know I made a big mistake blaming you for my problems, especially thinking you were like Lisa."

Josie glanced away, but Travis touched her cheek and made her look at him. "You're nothing like her. I was a fool to even think that. I'm crazy about you, Josie."

Josie pulled away, then rolled over to the other side and got up. She had to get away. He didn't love her, and she wouldn't fall into that trap like her mother had. Sooner or later, Travis would resent her and the baby. "It would never work between us," she said calmly.

He stood, too, then came around the bed. Panic

overtook her as she looked for a place to escape, but Travis cornered her. "Why?" he asked "Is it the baby? Do you think that I couldn't love a child that wasn't my own?"

She couldn't listen any longer. She pushed around him and went to the door and opened it. If he stayed a second longer, she was going to blurt out her feelings. "Please, Travis. I'm sorry, but I can't do this anymore. You need to leave."

He looked crushed but did as she asked and started to walk out. But before Josie could get the door closed, he put his hand up and his eyes flashed with anger. "Before I go, I just want you to know something, Josie. There's no one who could love you as much as I do. But if you're willing to throw that away..."

Josie's heart began to drum in her chest. Had she heard him right? "What did you say?"

"I said you're willing to throw that away."

She shook her head. "No, before that."

Travis's features softened as if he caught on to the depth of his confession. Then he took a step toward her and pulled her into his arms. His head lowered. "Oh, God, Josie, I love you." His mouth came down on hers in a kiss hungry with desire, telling her all the things that got messed up with words. His tongue pushed inside her mouth, caressing and stroking her lovingly. When he finally broke off, he rained kisses over her face.

Josie cupped his face, her eyes searching his. "I love you, Travis. I thought I was going to die if you walked away."

"Then why did you ask me to leave?"

"Because I needed your love," she said. "My

mother spent most of her life with a man she didn't love, wishing she could be with Hank. I wouldn't tell Hank, but I rarely saw her happy. I think she never got over loving him. Like I could never get over loving you.''

Travis's hold tightened on her. He couldn't believe how close he'd come to losing her. "You don't have to ever worry about that. I love you so much and that's never going to change." His forehead met hers as his hand covered her stomach. "And the baby, too. This kid is going to be a Randell."

More tears filled her eyes and that worried him.

"Is that a problem?" he asked.

She shook her head. "You're a wonderful man, Travis Randell."

"Just keep thinking that." He grinned and took her hand as he walked to the door. He stuck his fingers in his mouth and let out a sharp whistle. Soon Rocky trotted up to the porch. "Good, boy," he crooned to the animal and climbed on. "C'mon, Josie," he said as he held out his hand. "We need to tell the family about your new living arrangements."

She didn't move from the porch. "And just what living arrangements are those?"

Travis froze, suddenly realizing what she was asking. "Come here and I'll tell you. I guarantee you and the baby are going to like them."

She didn't look convinced as she made her way to the horse. Travis reached down and pulled her up. She sat in the saddle in front of him, then took the reins, and they headed back toward the valley. They rode though the grove of trees and looked out to the high grass and saw the herd of ponies still there. He stopped and turned Josie slightly toward him.

"I love you, Josie Gutierrez. From the moment I saw you here in the valley, I haven't been able to get you out of my head. Now you're in my heart. I want you by my side always. I want to share everything with you. Your sadness, your joy and I promise that no matter what, I will always be there for you. And you'd make me the happiest guy in the world if you'll marry me."

She nodded as tears filled her eyes. They were both remembering how close they'd come to losing each other. "I promise I will always love you, too, Travis. Yes, I'll marry you."

He leaned down and kissed her as the soft autumn breeze caressed them. Rocky shifted and Travis lifted his head and let out a yell that echoed his joy throughout the valley.

He smiled at her. "I guess we better start back to the house and tell the family." But just as they turned Rocky west three horsemen, Hank, Chance and Cade, came over the rise.

"Oh, boy, I better do some fast talking," Travis said. "Looks like your daddy and brothers are coming to rescue you."

Josie's eyes twinkled. "I guess I'll have to tell them I've already been rescued."

Travis's chest swelled with a love he'd never known existed. This was the real thing. Josie was the woman he needed to fill the empty spot in his heart. Together, they would heal the years of loneliness and fill their future with love.

He leaned down and kissed her, not caring that his family would see them. All that was on his mind was Josie.

The three riders reined in their mounts far enough

away not to disturb the couple. "Guess they didn't need our help after all," Chance said.

Cade leaned his arm on the saddle horn. "Yeah, I guess you can head off to Midland now. From the looks of it, I'd say our little brother is doing just fine without our help."

"Looks like we better get back and tell Ellà there's going to be another wedding." Hank grinned. "This time I get to give away the bride."

Epilogue

"She's beautiful," Travis said, as he held his new daughter in his arms. The hour-old baby was a perfect duplicate of Josie with a head full of black hair and big light-colored eyes.

"Yes, she is," Josie said, adjusting her position in the hospital bed. "I'll even forgive her for being so stubborn and taking twelve hours to be born."

Travis looked at his wife of six months. He couldn't love her any more than he did at this moment. She had given him so much. He sat down on the bed next to her. "I love you, Josie Randell. And I love this little one, too."

Josie's eyes met his. "And I love you. Sometimes I can't believe it's possible to be this happy. Life is perfect."

"It's pretty damn close," he agreed.

Josie leaned forward and peeked at the sleeping baby. "Maybe there is one thing. We could use a bigger place. The cabin's going to get pretty cozy with the three of us."

Travis liked cozy. They had decided to stay at the cabin after they married just weeks after he'd proposed. But with the guest ranch in full swing and the new baby, they had to move. "Hank's offered us the house," he said.

Josie shook her head. "No, I'm not going to move Dad out of his home. And you know he won't consider living with us."

Travis's heart warmed every time she called Hank, Dad. In the past months, father and daughter had only gotten closer. "Let's not worry about it now. Besides, I have a few ideas that might solve the problem."

Josie raised an eyebrow. "And what are those?"

Travis leaned over and kissed his wife, letting his lips linger on hers, just enjoying her sweetness. With a groan, he finally pulled back. "Lady, it's going to be hard to keep my hands off you for six weeks."

"You're trying to distract me from the question."

"Is it working?" he asked.

"Always," she said as a knock on the door made them separate.

Hank peeked into the room. "Can a grandpa see his new granddaughter?"

"You sure can," Josie said. "But first her mama needs a kiss."

Travis watched the two embrace. He still felt a little twinge of sadness remembering how he tried to keep them apart. How thankful he was that he'd come to his senses and given them a chance to be father and daughter.

A grinning Hank held his granddaughter in his arm. "She's a mighty pretty thing. Yes, you are," he crooned to the baby. "And Grandpa Hank's gonna buy you anything you want. How about a pony, a pretty spotted one?"

Josie shot a panicked glance at her husband. Travis smiled and gave her a reassuring nod, letting her know that he would handle the situation. She looked relieved. He loved his new role as protector of both his ladies. "Hey, Hank, maybe we should wait a few years for a horse. I bet she'd like a stuffed one."

Hank continued his conversation with the infant. "Well, how about that then, would you like a cuddly pony...?" He looked up at the parents. "What's this little one's name?"

Travis took Josie's hand. They shared a private smile, then he turned to Hank. "Her name is Elissa Mae Randell."

Three months later, Hank sat on horseback as he looked over Mustang Valley. Just like forty years before, he was in awe of the beauty that had brought him here to live and raise cattle and a family. He smiled as he tipped his hat back. What a family he had. The three sons he'd raised and loved as if they were his own. A daughter that was a surprise blessing. His two daughters-in-law and the four grandkids at present count were a very welcome addition. Things had certainly changed this past year. The Mustang Valley Guest Ranch was open now. Amazingly, he found he liked having people around, liked telling stories about the mustangs at the campfires.

Life had been good to him, and he knew that his sons were going to teach their children what was important in life. Family. He was just glad he was a part of it.

The sound of trucks on the road drew Hank's attention. He turned as three vehicles parked where the road stopped. They were here.

Josie and Travis were the first ones to climb out with little Elissa. Next was Cade and Abby's new red Suburban that had Mustang Valley Guest Ranch printed on the side. They got out along with Brandon and their new baby, James Henry, born just a month after his cousin. Chance and Joy pulled up in a black crew-cab Ford. Ella opened the back door and got out carrying Katie Rose.

The housekeeper came down the rise. "Well, what's so all-fired important that you had to have us all here?"

"Is it a crime to want the family together?" Hank asked.

The three men he'd called his sons for the past twenty years stood with their families. Hank had to pause and just enjoy it.

"Is there something wrong, Hank?" Chance asked.

Hank shook his head and glanced toward the valley to see the herd of mustangs grazing peacefully. That was how he felt. Peaceful. "No, Chance, everything is fine. I just wanted to discuss some family matters. You all know that I turned over the Circle B to the three of you boys." With their nods he continued, "but that was before I discovered my daughter."

Josie immediately came forward. "No, Hank, please, I don't want to change anything."

His daughter was as stubborn as they came, and he couldn't be prouder. "Don't you know not to argue with your elders, young lady? Now just let me say my piece. I'm not changing anything. Chance, Cade and Travis own the Circle B. But I did keep a special piece of land.'' He climbed down from his horse and went to Josie. He placed his hand on her shoulders and turned her toward the valley and the high spring grass that backed up to the hills. ''See that section between the hills—'' he moved his hand to the east ''—and the creek?''

''I see it. It's beautiful. I have taken several photos.''

''Well, it's about twenty acres, and it goes all the way back to the highway.'' He swallowed. ''I want you to have it. That's where I want you and Travis to build your home.''

Josie gasped. ''Oh, Hank, no. I can't.''

''I won't take no for answer,'' he said stubbornly. ''It's my gift to give to you. If you don't take it, I'm going to have to change my will and redefine the shares of the Circle B.''

Tears filled Josie's eyes as she glanced at her husband. When Travis gave her his nod, she looked back at Hank. ''Oh, Dad, you've given me so much.''

Hank pulled Josie into his arms. ''Oh, Josie girl, you're the one who has given to me.''

She pulled back from the embrace. ''I love you.''

''And I love you.'' He sniffed and gave her a gentle shove. ''Now, scoot off to your husband. I believe he has some house plans to discuss with you.''

Josie gave him a quick kiss then went running into Travis's arms. Hank watched. It did him good to see her so happy. He didn't even mind losing his newly found daughter to a man like Travis. In fact, all three Randell men were something special. He'd like to think he had a hand in that.

Ella walked up. ''You're pretty proud of yourself, aren't you?'' she asked Hank. They both had their eyes on the boys. The boys they raised when everyone else had given up on them. Hank had never even thought about doing that.

"I'm pretty proud of them. I want to thank you, Ella, for loving them, too."

Ella blinked her eyes, obviously surprised by his compliment. "That was the easy part."

"No, this is the easy part. We get to spoil the grandkids."

Ella hugged little Katie in her arms. "I've already got a head start on you. I kind of like being Grandma Ella."

Hank looked out at his valley. He knew that his children would look after the mustangs, just as he'd taught them. They would always have a home here.

Along with the generation of children to come.

* * * * *

**Separated at birth,
reunited by a mysterious bequest,
these triplet sisters discover
a legacy of love!**

THE WEDDING LEGACY

A brand-new series coming to
Silhouette Romance from heartwarming author

CARA COLTER

Available July 2001:
HUSBAND BY INHERITANCE (SR #1532)

Available August 2001:
THE HEIRESS TAKES A HUSBAND (SR #1538)

Available September 2001:
WED BY A WILL (SR #1544)

Available at your favorite retail outlet.

Silhouette®
Where love comes alive™

Visit Silhouette at www.eHarlequin.com   SRTWL

Silhouette®

where love comes alive—online...

eHARLEQUIN.com

your romantic escapes

—Indulgences—

♥ Monthly guides to indulging yourself, such as:
  ★ Tub Time: A guide for bathing beauties
  ★ Magic Massages: A treat for tired feet

—Horoscopes—

♥ Find your daily Passionscope, weekly Lovescopes and Erotiscopes

♥ Try our compatibility game

—Reel Love—

♥ Read all the latest romantic movie reviews

—Royal Romance—

♥ Get the latest scoop on your favorite royal romances

—Romantic Travel—

♥ For the most romantic destinations, hotels and travel activities

All this and more available at
www.eHarlequin.com
on Women.com Networks

SINTE1R

If you enjoyed what you just read,
then we've got an offer you can't resist!

Take 2 bestselling love stories FREE!

Plus get a FREE surprise gift!

Clip this page and mail it to Silhouette Reader Service™

IN U.S.A.
3010 Walden Ave.
P.O. Box 1867
Buffalo, N.Y. 14240-1867

IN CANADA
P.O. Box 609
Fort Erie, Ontario
L2A 5X3

YES! Please send me 2 free Silhouette Romance® novels and my free surprise gift. After receiving them, if I don't wish to receive anymore, I can return the shipping statement marked cancel. If I don't cancel, I will receive 6 brand-new novels every month, before they're available in stores! In the U.S.A., bill me at the bargain price of $3.15 plus 25¢ shipping and handling per book and applicable sales tax, if any*. In Canada, bill me at the bargain price of $3.50 plus 25¢ shipping and handling per book and applicable taxes**. That's the complete price and a savings of at least 10% off the cover prices—what a great deal! I understand that accepting the 2 free books and gift places me under no obligation ever to buy any books. I can always return a shipment and cancel at any time. Even if I never buy another book from Silhouette, the 2 free books and gift are mine to keep forever.

215 SEN DFNQ
315 SEN DFNR

Name	(PLEASE PRINT)	
Address	Apt.#	
City	State/Prov.	Zip/Postal Code

* Terms and prices subject to change without notice. Sales tax applicable in N.Y.
** Canadian residents will be charged applicable provincial taxes and GST.
   All orders subject to approval. Offer limited to one per household and not valid to
   current Silhouette Romance® subscribers.
® are registered trademarks of Harlequin Enterprises Limited.

SROM01   ©1998 Harlequin Enterprises Limited

SILHOUETTE®
MAKES YOU
A STAR!

Feel like a star with Silhouette.

**We will fly you and a guest to New York City for an
exciting weekend stay at a glamorous 5-star hotel.
Experience a refreshing day at one of New York's
trendiest spas and have your photo taken by a
professional. Plus, receive $1,000 U.S. spending money!**

**Flowers...long walks...dinner for two...
how does Silhouette Books
make romance come alive for you?**

Send us a script, with 500 words or less, along with visuals (only drawings,
magazine cutouts or photographs or combination thereof). Show us how
Silhouette Makes Your Love Come Alive. Be creative and have fun. No
purchase necessary. All entries must be clearly marked with your name,
address and telephone number. All entries will become property of
Silhouette and are not returnable. **Contest closes September 28, 2001.**

Please send your entry to: **Silhouette Makes You a Star!**

In U.S.A.	In Canada
P.O. Box 9069	P.O. Box 637
Buffalo, NY, 14269-9069	Fort Erie, ON, L2A 5X3

Look for contest details on the next page, by visiting www.eHarlequin.com or
request a copy by sending a self-addressed envelope to the applicable address
above. Contest open to Canadian and U.S. residents who are 18 or over.
Void where prohibited.

Silhouette®
Where love comes alive™

Our lucky winner's photo will appear in a Silhouette ad. Join the fun!

SRMYAS1

HARLEQUIN "SILHOUETTE MAKES YOU A STAR!" CONTEST 1308
OFFICIAL RULES
NO PURCHASE NECESSARY TO ENTER

1. To enter, follow directions published in the offer to which you are responding. Contest begins June 1, 2001, and ends on September 28, 2001. Entries must be postmarked by September 28, 2001, and received by October 5, 2001. Enter by hand-printing (or typing) on an 8 ½" x 11" piece of paper your name, address (including zip code), contest number/name and attaching a script containing 500 words or less, along with drawings, photographs or magazine cutouts, or combinations thereof (i.e., collage) on no larger than 9" x 12" piece of paper, describing how the Silhouette books make romance come alive for you. Mail via first-class mail to: Harlequin "Silhouette Makes You a Star!" Contest 1308, (in the U.S.) P.O. Box 9069, Buffalo, NY 14269-9069, (in Canada) P.O. Box 637, Fort Erie, Ontario, Canada L2A 5X3. Limit one entry per person, household or organization.

2. Contests will be judged by a panel of members of the Harlequin editorial, marketing and public relations staff. Fifty percent of criteria will be judged against script and fifty percent will be judged against drawing, photographs and/or magazine cutouts. Judging criteria will be based on the following:

   - Sincerity—25%
   - Originality and Creativity—50%
   - Emotionally Compelling—25%

   In the event of a tie, duplicate prizes will be awarded. Decisions of the judges are final.

3. All entries become the property of Torstar Corp. and may be used for future promotional purposes. Entries will not be returned. No responsibility is assumed for lost, late, illegible, incomplete, inaccurate, nondelivered or misdirected mail.

4. Contest open only to residents of the U.S. (except Puerto Rico) and Canada who are 18 years of age or older, and is void wherever prohibited by law; all applicable laws and regulations apply. Any litigation within the Province of Quebec respecting the conduct or organization of a publicity contest may be submitted to the Régie des alcools, des courses et des jeux for a ruling. Any litigation respecting the awarding of a prize may be submitted to the Régie des alcools, des courses et des jeux only for the purpose of helping the parties reach a settlement. Employees and immediate family members of Torstar Corp. and D. L. Blair, Inc., their affiliates, subsidiaries and all other agencies, entities and persons connected with the use, marketing or conduct of this contest are not eligible to enter. Taxes on prizes are the sole responsibility of the winner. Acceptance of any prize offered constitutes permission to use winner's name, photograph or other likeness for the purposes of advertising, trade and promotion on behalf of Torstar Corp., its affiliates and subsidiaries without further compensation to the winner, unless prohibited by law.

5. Winner will be determined no later than November 30, 2001, and will be notified by mail. Winner will be required to sign and return an Affidavit of Eligibility/Release of Liability/Publicity Release form within 15 days after winner notification. Noncompliance within that time period may result in disqualification and an alternative winner may be selected. All travelers must execute a Release of Liability prior to ticketing and must possess required travel documents (e.g., passport, photo ID) where applicable. Trip must be booked by December 31, 2001, and completed within one year of notification. No substitution of prize permitted by winner. Torstar Corp. and D. L. Blair, Inc., their parents, affiliates and subsidiaries are not responsible for errors in printing of contest, entries and/or game pieces. In the event of printing or other errors that may result in unintended prize values or duplication of prizes, all affected game pieces or entries shall be null and void. **Purchase or acceptance of a product offer does not improve your chances of winning.**

6. Prizes: (1) Grand Prize—A 2-night/3-day trip for two (2) to New York City, including round-trip coach air transportation nearest winner's home and hotel accommodations (double occupancy) at The Plaza Hotel, a glamorous afternoon makeover at a trendy New York spa, $1,000 in U.S. spending money and an opportunity to have a professional photo taken and appear in a Silhouette advertisement (approximate retail value: $7,000). (10) Ten Runner-Up Prizes of gift packages (retail value $50 ea.). Prizes consist of only those items listed as part of the prize. Limit one prize per person. Prize is valued in U.S. currency.

7. For the name of the winner (available after December 31, 2001) send a self-addressed, stamped envelope to: Harlequin "Silhouette Makes You a Star!" Contest 1197 Winners, P.O. Box 4200 Blair, NE 68009-4200 or you may access the www.eHarlequin.com Web site through February 28, 2002.

Contest sponsored by Torstar Corp., P.O Box 9042, Buffalo, NY 14269-9042.

SRMYAS2